SHORT TALES

By Alex Starke

Published by Five Jacks Publishing
Eugene, Oregon, USA

ISBN-13: 978-0-9862909-2-3

Cover and book design by Anne Starke
www.starkeconcepts.com

This book is dedicated to my wonderful wife, Anne. The best supporter, greatest critic, major cheerleader, and best friend one could have in life. And, of course, to Thor, my inspirational Jack Russell.

TABLE OF CONTENTS

Would You Like to Place an Order Now? 7

Mr. Tidley Meets the Boneman .17

Hearth and Home 33

The Big Accidental Bump 39

A Normal World 63

A New Beginning 69

Heart's Wish 107

Mr. Tidley and the Boneman:
In Pursuit of the Black Chicken III

About the Author 147

WOULD YOU LIKE TO PLACE AN ORDER NOW?

Quint Solfanger sincerely hoped he was the last to arrive for the big occasion. He entered through the unguarded stadium door and quickly mixed into the bustling throng of people on the arena floor. He scanned the crowd and estimated it numbered close to a thousand or more. All wore shirts and hats for and against various peoples and parties. Literally everyone held signs and banners that screamed the name of their fearless leader, President Lügner (Lug) Widerlich.

Quint worked his way to a point near the front of the stage where a group of burly men stood to keep the exuberant crowd back. He found a spot nearby where he could observe his intended target and the followers before making a final decision. Quint waited impatiently for the show to begin.

Soon a slick-looking man stepped up to the podium and began to speak an introduction.

"Hello and welcome. How wonderful to see such a big turnout tonight, a big night for us Luggers and – "

Quint made mental notes as he observed the cheering, jostling, and hooting people. He hoped he would not have to wait much longer for the big moment – there was the damned parking lot incident to consider and if that was noticed it could really muck up his plan.

Finally, the speaker ended his spiel.

"Okay folks, enough of me talking. I know why you've come, and who you want to see. So, without any further delay, here he is, our man in the White House and Godsend to the country, Lug Widerlich!"

The crowd went wild with applause and shouts as a big man with a tanned face and well-styled hair strode confidently onto the stage. Quint noticed with amusement that a few women (and men) began to swoon and faint. Widerlich stepped up to the podium and raised his arms over his head, hands clasped together in a self-congratulatory manner. He waited while his jubilant followers roared and stamped their feet. Finally he lowered his arms and held up the palms of his hands to his ecstatic audience. Everyone in the arena knew the drill; it was time to quiet down.

Lug Widerlich smiled broadly.

"Hello, people! How are my fans tonight? I can tell you how I'm doing and how the country is doing tonight – tremendously wonderful!"

The crowd burst into more frantic applause and cheering.

Widerlich held up his hands again for quiet.

"I've come here tonight to speak about our enemies, the country's enemies. The people who have no interest in you and are hell-bent on destroying me with their fake – "

Quint heard a shout from the back of the arena. "Widerlich is a crook and is destroying the country. Lock him up, lock him up, lock him – "

Quint turned and saw a man in the upper level being punched by the people surrounding him. Finally, four men grabbed the screaming, bloodied heckler and made to throw him off the upper level.

"Okay, that's enough," Widerlich commanded. The men stopped.

"That's right, put him down now. Thanks for showing such loyalty, guys. These people always try to break up my speeches with their lies, but you guys always step in. Thanks."

Widerlich smiled a thin hard smile.

"Now get him out of here. Don't be too gentle now – when he is outside, who knows what could happen to him?"

He laughed as the protester was shoved, kicked, and punched out the door. Quint saw a determined man in bib overalls follow him outside.

Widerlich sketched a mock salute to the closing door.

"Adios amigo. As I was saying. We all have to – "

The man who had followed the protester burst back into the upper level.

"There's a goddamn spaceship out in the parking lot. Holy shit, you gotta – "

"Hey up there," shouted Widerlich, "Who's giving the speech, halfwit? Me or you?"

The man hesitated. "But it's true. Darn thing crushed the whole front end of my pickup truck and – "

Damnation! Quint thought, but then was relieved when several black clad security people hastily grabbed the man and clapped a bag over his head before dragging him away.

▸▸ ▸▸ ▸▸

The man – one Rufus Buckshot from Blue Ridge, Georgia – was found years later by his wife, Dolores, in Smolensk, working as a conductor second-class on the inner-city commuter tram. Saturday nights he moonlighted as a symbolic interpretive dancer at Club Moskva. When confronted by his wife while performing on stage, he ran away in terror screaming, 'Ham sandwich and soup!' After his escape he eventually settled down as a flamenco guitarist in an obscure sherry bar outside of Madrid, playing for drinks and tips.

◄◄ ◄◄ ◄◄

After the reluctant Rufus was carried out of sight, Lügner Widerlich smiled and continued, "Don't listen to him, people. No such a thing as climate change or UFOs, big opposition plot, that's all. Now settle down."

He continued his speech to the faithful, delivering his usual greatest hits that were red meat for his adoring minions. Chants of *Build that moat!* and *Lock up the Europeans!* rocked the hall. Quint closed his eyes – absorbing all the rancor and rage that was thick as a noxious fog around him – and made his decision. He glanced down at the small widget on his belt that had a series of tiny studs. *Diversion time*, he thought, and began to laugh loudly. A couple nearby who had matching shirts that read "Ignorance is Bliss" looked at him and began to frown in puzzlement.

Quint shouted at the man on stage.

"Ach, what a pretentious boor you are."

Widerlich paused – his face turning a bit red – and looked down in his direction. "What did you say?"

"Oh, sorry. I did say you were a pretentious boor, but

upon reflection it was a bit of an understatement. I should have said you were an apple-faced, half-witted baboon, with pine sap for a brain, who is vying to become a pretentious boor. Will that suffice, you bloviating stench from an elephant's hindquarters?"

There was a hush over the entire arena. Widerlich's eyes looked as if they could spout hellfire. The moment was brief – Widerlich pointed at him.

"Get that guy and throw him out!"

With a collective roar, the crowd and security guys surged towards him. Quint calmly punched a stud on the widget. The Rejexit Mark V protective screen surrounded him with a faint purple shimmer – the mob converged.

A hairy man with a huge gut tried to grip Quint in a bear hug. He was immediately catapulted back at the surrounding throng. On his outward trajectory he bowled over a few dozen angry people – including a toothless grandpa who had a pink-iced donut with sprinkles fiercely clenched in his gums.

One of the black-clad security men, Sammy Fracker, was next. He tried to clout Quint with a baton, but the club rebounded back at Sammy's head with such force he dropped like a sack of mildewed potatoes.

▶▶ ▶▶ ▶▶

Sammy came out of his self-inflicted coma a month later and promptly ran away with a wandering troupe of performing Jack Russell terriers, where he achieved a modicum of fame as the singing fire-hydrant.

◀◀ ◀◀ ◀◀

Others tried to attack Quint, all were repelled like

popcorn exploding on a hot buttered griddle. A wide angry circle finally cleared around him. One guy took a shot at Quint with a pistol. The bullet ricocheted away and blew up the poor pink-iced donut with sprinkles that the grandpa still held clamped in his gums. The sprinkles shot everywhere and temporarily blinded Doris Raymond from Slapout, Oklahoma. Hands clasped over her sprinkle-shot eyes, she ran in a panic, unfortunately straight into one of the huge wooden columns supporting the upper level of the arena.

▶▶ ▶▶ ▶▶

Doris woke up three days later, her sight restored. She proclaimed it a miracle, telling the bemused medical staff she had been visited by a large cheese blintz in flowing robes who had told her the true purpose of life. The next day she moved to San Francisco and became a shaman living in a large cardboard box in an alley near Market Street. Her ardent followers include two calico cats, a dog named Klinkers, and beat patrolman Mulvaney.

◀◀ ◀◀ ◀◀

Grandpa – remnants of the mortally wounded pink-iced donut spattered on his enraged face – jumped on the pistol wielding guy and began to chomp on his neck. The man screamed and dropped the pistol which immediately went off. The bullet hit a control panel that promptly dropped Lug Widerlich's speech-ending grand finale balloons and glitter on his followers. The entire crowd of *Luggers* erupted in rage and attacked one another in outraged frustration over such an abbreviated ranting from their dear leader.

The throng now ignoring him, Quint pushed another stud and popped up on stage next to the stunned President. He smiled sunnily at him.

"Well that worked out well now didn't it? Ready to go?"

Widerlich recovered himself quickly. "Go where? I not going anywhere, dimbulb."

He pointed an index finger at Quint.

"And just who the hell are you? You're going to pay for making me look ridiculous in front of the rubes."

Quint laughed. "Oh no, my fine specimen. It is I who will be paid, and handsomely. You see, I am Quint Solfanger, a collector and supplier of – "

Widerlich bellowed. "Doesn't matter. When my people are done with you, you won't be collecting anything but a disability check. That is, until I cut the funding for that program."

He signaled to a group of men at the back of the stage sporting long truncheons who quickly came out and surrounded Quint. Smiling, they raised their clubs to strike – Quint pushed another stud and vanished with the President. With their boss and intended victim gone, the frustrated thugs fell on each other in blind fury amidst the drifting balloons and softly falling glitter.

A member of the audience, Rob Tuppy – who had paused from bludgeoning a fellow Lugger with a ceramic statue of Widerlich – saw the scene unfold.

▸▸ ▸▸ ▸▸

Years later working as a headwaiter at a Denny's in Billings, Montana, Rob would recount that it was 'The finest dang finale he ever had the privilege of attending.'

Lug Widerlich woke up inside of what appeared to be a very large canning jar. Quint was looking in at him.

"Perfect, awake at last. Welcome aboard my craft. Sorry you weren't conscious for the journey, I'm sure the conversation would have been quite amusing. Anyway, I've got you all packaged up and ready for pickup."

Widerlich stood up and said, "Pickup? Come on, let's make a deal. Let me out now and I'll cut you in on my action. The money is huge, believe me, these people will buy into anything I tell them."

Quint shook his head and said, "As I began telling you earlier; I am a collector and supplier of fine delicacies to only the most discerning tastes of the galaxy. I have to say that until I heard about you, I was going to grab a rotting Mammoth corpse that had been defrosting in the Siberian tundra for a few months. My clients, you see, are the Croobezk, who are the inhabitants of the planet Odious Kugelfang. We have just made a landing near their capital city and they are coming to take delivery. The Croobezk are desirous of – "

He paused and turned as a large door behind him opened. Widerlich looked past him and his tan faded to the shade of vanilla.

Quint said, "Ah, here they are now. Now, as I was saying, they are desirous of something new, totally revolting, filthy, and disgusting. Something that will pair well with a finely aged glass of Plexion goat sweat. You, are, shall we say, a sample for their edification."

Widerlich screamed and beat against the glass as he was hauled away by large wasp-like beings with nasty looking mandibles.

A day later a Croobezk with scintillating hues of green and purple on its carapace came to visit Quint at his ship.

"Greetings trader," it lisped in a low buzz. "I must tell you the specimen you provided was unusually awful. So foul and reeking – we all loved it, especially the head, which was so ecstatically horrid and went so well with a warmed stein of Rolfgut twizzle. May I enquire what they are called, and if you have a further supply of these disgusting delicacies?"

Quint stopped counting the gold bars he had received for his cargo and smiled broadly at the creature.

"Oh yes, there are more. They call them supreme leaders or dictators, and if I run out of them, there are always the followers. They are not quite as rancid as this one, but still fairly repulsive and repugnant. Would you like to place an order now?"

MR. TIDLEY MEETS THE BONEMAN

It had been a slow day in my establishment, but it was early yet. Yawning, I brought out the Gabbler to view the latest chatter around the universe, as always keeping one eye on the infernal device and the other on the entrance to my bar. There was an interesting story on one of the outer galactic planets called Medivus Rex that caused my ears to prick up. I imagined from the name it was one of those romanticized throwback orbits where everyone lived in a Middle-Ages scenario. Lots of blood, swords, more blood, and sumptuous amounts of body odor. Anyway, there was an unusual knight who challenged in single combat, to the death, any who sought egress to his boss's castle. The knight had been on an impressive winning streak; body counts were piling up, and...damn! In stormed someone whose scaly visage I could have done without seeing today – Blaithon Zweee.

I reached under the bar and put a wicked Vauxhall dagger in my paw. Blaithon was an Umvornian, a particularly ugly standout amongst a remarkably hideous reptilian species – I was taking no chances.

He swaggered up to the bar, towering over me, and said, "Tidley, I'm gonna take those loopy ears of yours and tie them in a Crallus knot! Then I'll stick yer damn nub of a tail up where the sun don't shine!"

Umvornian speech sounds like an endless stream of wet gas blobs impacting a wall at high speed, but with my implanted Skritstone the muddle translated sufficiently enough into Stellar Standard. The idea of hearing a roomful of these ugly buggers talking at once made me shiver. Ghastly thought.

I put away the Gabbler, looked up at his yellowed face. "That is *Mr.* Tidley to you Zweee, and what may I ask has gotten your sphincter in such an uproar?"

"Don't gimme any verkshit, Tidley! You know good and well what. I got my six-hundred CelCreds stolen here last night. I'm getting em' back right now!"

He reached across the bar for me with a large grease splattered hand, each digit sporting a dagger talon. I waited until the last second, then the Vauxhall flashed, separating the dirty nailed appendage from its owner. I stepped aside as it bounced off behind the bar. One nice thing about Vauxhalls is that they cut through anything like simi-butter, and cauterize at the same time. Nice, clean, and no bloody mess to clean up afterwards. Quite handy in this case, as the ichor that runs through these buggers's veins smells akin to a jellied Vlotfish left out in the sun too long. One whiff would drop a whole herd of Titan buffaloes in an instant.

Shrieking, the Umvornian fell to his knees, grasping the stump of his wrist. I didn't say Vauxhalls are painless, did I? Not a chance. I jumped over the bar next to him now that he was down on my level. Zweee's eyes widened in fear, feeling the razor edge of molecularly enhanced steel on his throat. The shrieking died away to a whimper.

I put my muzzle next to his face and lifted my lips, exposing sharp canines. "The name is *Mr.* Tidley, you ill-favored, malodorous, Plink-twaddler! Never forget that. You've quite a nerve coming in here threatening me. Search that gelatinous mass of stinking goo in your ugly head, and remember last night, drunk as a dungball plotz, you lost all your CelCreds at the Vaktu table. It is not my affair if you had unfavorable tiles in the game."

He muttered something about being cheated, but I cut him off...no, not with the blade! "Not another word out of you, Blaithon!" I pressed the edge harder into a fold of his flaking, yellow scaled neck. "I run a tight ship here and nobody will have the audacity to name me a cheat, especially a grease-spattered, ratty-scaled, petard as you." I held him in my gaze for a moment, then said, "You may leave now with your life if you so choose, or I can end you – to me it is a matter of complete indifference. If you decide that you wish to keep living, leave at once, and never dirty my establishment with your one-handed presence again. Do you perceive my meaning, twaddle-brain?"

He nodded, so I backed away while he got up and shambled towards the front door.

I jumped back on my raised platform behind the bar and nearly stumbled over something lying there. I picked it up... "Oh, Blaithon. You forgot something." Zweee turned, and his severed appendage smacked him in the face.

There are days like that around here. Most, though, were becoming quite a bore.

Tidley's Tale

The Stinking Pilgrim is on the main thoroughfare in the raucous outpost of Blaxstadde ve Tardre. The city is a lively little whistle-stop on planet Guillaume 9, the gateway to the outer orbits, and occupied by any kind of character imaginable. Most are transient chancers looking to move on quickly to make a mark on the wild territorial and themed worlds that comprise the vast swirl called the outer orbits. The balance is a collection of spacer pilots waiting on the next job, and those of dubious background waiting to prey upon the unsuspecting traveler.

There are, of course, a contingent of Centurionem lawkeepers from the Central Unity of Peace and Intergalactic Egalitarian Sanguinity (CUPIES), but their presence here is small. Guillaume 9 is on the frontier of CUPIES authority, though they would love to incorporate it fully into their ever-enlarging family of races and planets. Let's just say that they will not have an easy time of assimilating old Guillaume 9.

Me, well, I come from a rare and ancient race called Hundogca. My kind are descended from the noble house, Jacks Russell. Doesn't ring any bells? Well that is not surprising.

My forebears came from a planet way off the galactic charts called Earth. From what the Hist-Holos say we arrived thousands of years ago, right after the Big Accidental Bump occurred. That's a long story however – perhaps to be told another time. Suffice it to say that the Heralds of CUPIES made an approach to Earth with their huge craft, hoping to invite the inhabitants into their fraternity. Due to a nervous Herald captain and a few unfortunate missile launches by the locals from their primitive spaceships, the Earth was destroyed completely.

While the Heralds were navigating hastily out of the system, they happened upon Earth's lone settlement in space – a small mining colony on Mars. Realizing that the poor creatures would likely perish due to a lack of supply ships coming from Earth, the Heralds decided to act. Not wanting to risk any shenanigans from the colony, they sleep-blasted the whole lot from orbit, then ventured down and loaded up every living being. All of them were ferried back to the ship and stored in stasis. The Heralds made their way back to CUPIES Central to have the upper pay grades sort everything out.

The cargo was eventually given to the department of Central Relocation of Alien Persons (CRAP) who began investigating what they found to be three species. The first ones examined were the humans. When put through the analysis scans, they were found to be pretty much on a par with most bi-pedal races – though perhaps less pleasant to look upon. Further scanning of their reasoning and higher function levels set off the technician's alarm bells.

The humans were found to display eccentric levels of behavior that would not be suitable to the highly cultured inner civilization of CUPIES. It was decided to ship the humans to an outer planet, then bring them up to speed via edu-implants so they could cope in their new galactic environment. They were outfitted with ships, technology, and other supplies, pointed in the direction of the wild outer orbits and told to go forth and propagate. The humans took the proverbial bit in their mouths and ran with it. At present, there are more than one thousand human-run worlds in the outer orbits.

After the humans had been shipped off, there remained two other species that perplexed CRAP – the Hundogca and the Kattze. There were fewer of them, and the technicians could not understand the reasoning characteristics of their brains: lack of coherent speech, useful hands, and especially the inability to walk on two legs as the humans did. After many meetings with top CRAP bureau anchors, it was decided that both species were undoubtedly a slave race to the humans who had been intentionally disabled. CRAP decided to put the indignity to rights and sent them to the reframe bubble tanks.

You could pretty much say that both came out as new races. They could now speak and walk on two legs, if they wished. They were endowed with front paws that were prehensile with opposable thumbs. Their brains had been re-modified and enlarged, which, coupled with the old senses and cunning instincts, made them quite formidable. Unfortunately, all of their previously long tails were reduced in size to little nubs. CRAP apologized for that again and again, claiming it was an unexpected glitch in the bubble tanks. I'm sure having a long tail would have proved most useful for things like pointing, clearing tables, or whapping individuals in the face, but in the end they (the Hundogca at least) got over it.

The Kattze were secretive and kept to themselves. A few days after everyone had gone through the bit with the edu-implants, they broke out of their rooms at CRAP, hijacked an interstellar speed-yacht and disappeared. It was rumored they made it out to the Ve du Rys territories, a wild group of little-explored orbits.

The Hundogca are of five Houses: Shepherd, Labrador, Bouledogue, the foppish Pudelhund, and my honorable House Jacks Russell. The Hundogca reside in the CUPIES systems and in the outer orbits as well, each having their own particular specialties and professions. We Jacks are stubbornly independent, doing a myriad of things from accounting, freebooting, and even owning a bar in a territorial outpost.

Personally, I come from a checkered background. To some, many of my past occupations might seem questionable indeed, perhaps even bordering on the slightly illegal. Be that as it may, I am now a respectable businessman, having won the Pilgrim in a game of Pitted Snark with the former – and unfortunately deceased – owner.

Enter the Boneman

So anyway, after my little understanding with the Omvornian Zweee had been completed, I looked in the reflective to make sure I wasn't appearing disheveled in any way – have to keep up appearances, you know. I eyed myself critically, it seemed that I was getting a little too fat and complacent looking. I thought that perhaps – except for a few episodes like Zweee – life was becoming a bit too easy here.

I sighed and settled in again with one eye on the Gabbler, the other on the door to the Pilgrim. My ears pricked up once again over that story on Medivus Rex about the undefeated warrior who had the odd title of The Dung Knight. He seemed to be the sole defender of a highly-wanted criminal known as The Black Chicken. Odd, to be sure.

Hmmm, must be the words had a different meaning on that planet. I thought to myself smiling. No vid from the Gabbler though, because Medivus was one of those orbits that has forsaken modern technology. Only one area on the whole planet where it operated, and that was on its one small spaceport. The rest of the orbit had a damper field which rendered anything from grav-sleds to blasters into useless junk. Horses, armor, with the usual weaponry of the ancient Middle-Ages of Earth were the operant factors there. I also understood that magic was a distinct possibility.

I was still musing about this when my nose twitched. I smelled something that almost made me grab the Vauxhall again...a human was near. I set the Gabbler back down again with a sigh and watched the front door, paw near the dagger.

Within a minute or so, sure enough, in walked a tall specimen. He sported a loud neon pink shirt with shifting purple and maroon stripes. A bright red leather vest overlay this, along with a wide, many-pocketed turquoise belt. His pants were of a highly reflective silver type material that would be sure to blind anyone looking at him in the midday sun. These were tucked into a knee-high pair of tough black Grot hide boots. He was topped off by a wide brimmed black hat made of the same material as his footwear.

I moved my paw away from the dagger, grabbed a

highly illegal Feur Mark VII Ashmaker, quickly tucking the gun into a pouch in my apron. Only a certain type dressed like this – a bounty hunter.

He ambled up to the bar and said, "Afternoon."

I nodded. "Indeed it is. What is your pleasure, citizen?"

"How about some of Blaxstadde's finest ale? I'm on the parched side today."

I grabbed a glass from under the bar and proceeded to draw him a Gutbugger's ale. I was hoping there would be no trouble with him. I noticed he sported a Flinderbus D-I pistol on his belt, which was not a typical piece for one in his trade – too flashy and unreliable. It could be set to stun, or totally fry a person, but the D-I was well known for eccentric glitches. Well at least he hadn't made any moves for it. I relaxed a little, wondering if this one might be a showy amateur.

"One CelCred, if you please." I said placing the frothing vessel in front of him.

He flipped the required coin on the bar and took a long draught of the brew.

"Ahh, now that's just what I needed." He eyed me for a long moment with a hint of a smile on his face. "House of Jacks, right?"

"Correct." I replied.

"Dang. I thought so. I never met one of your kind before. Thought you all mostly stayed in the CUPIES orbits."

I grabbed a glass to polish. "Now you know different."

He took another pull from his ale, looked around and leaned in closer to the bar. "Say, you don't happen to know an Umvornian who goes by the moniker of Sivid Zwaak, do you?"

I stopped polishing and looked up at him. Sivid Zwaak was a real horror story. He made Blaithon Zweee look like a docile cow in comparison. I knew for a fact he was wanted on at least forty CUPIES worlds for various crimes ranging from strong-arm robberies to outright murder. In Blaxstadde he was the number two man for Curly Dorkat, the repugnant human who ran things of the illegal nature in this burg. Zwaak was also one of my regular customers. Not that I liked him at all, but CelCreds are CelCreds and a Jack does have bills to pay.

I studied the man's face for a moment. "And whom, may I ask, wants to know?"

"People call me Boneman."

"Boneman is it? You have business with Zwaak?"

He smiled. "Maybe, maybe not. Just have to see, I guess. Does he ever come in your place?"

"Occasionally." I paused, looking him up and down with a frown, then. "Mr. Bonehead, I trust you do not intend any mischief in my establishment if he does appear? That would not sit well with me at all." I stared at him hard. "Do we understand each other?"

He looked a little pained and said, "It's Boneman, like rib bone, thigh bone. Oh, no worries, no worries about any trouble. I just want to talk a little business with him, that's all." With that he winked, grabbed his ale, and made his way to a table in the rear of the bar.

I thought to myself that this guy really was an amateur. Coming in here and asking questions like that, with a positively outrageous nickname. Boneman indeed! Why, all of the pros I was acquainted with had real names like Glomp Spittlepot, Wilhemina Hackblade, or Ux Wanker.

The only exception I knew of was the dreadful and highly successful *PFFFLLTTT!*, who went by the nickname Big Jake Thunderbutt. No, most real professionals would have been much more surreptitious. They kept a low profile, did their business, and left quickly – this I knew from experience. I really hoped Sivid Zwaak would not be coming in today.

After about an hour had gone by the evening crowd started to arrive. I looked over at my character at the rear table, but he seemed to be nodding off. *Bonehead can't handle his ale,* I thought with a smile. Placing the Ashmaker back under the bar, my eyes went back to the front door – my smile disappeared. Coming directly at me was Sivid Zwaak and two of his hulking, warty Orgl associates. That's when things got interesting.

"Well, Mr. Tidley." He growled. "I heard you had an eventful day today." He narrowed his saurian yellow eyes. "That is, according to my associate, Blaithon Zweee."

Flitzing hell! I attempted to grab the Ashmaker, but one of the Orgls quickly had me by the throat, holding me dangling over the bar. This was not looking good. I heard the feet of many people exiting the bar... soon the room was quiet.

Zwaak gave me a nasty toothy smile and said. "Didn't realize he was one of ours, eh? Well that is really too bad for you." He nodded at the Orgl who slammed me onto the bar pinning my right arm outstretched. His other hairy arm was across my neck keeping me in place.

"He got what he deserved, Sivid, the bugger tried to put his squalid hand on me so I separated it from him." My brain was desperately trying to come up with something to get me out of this dilemma. I figured to keep talking to purchase some time.

"You know I run a straight up game of Vaktu here. Zweee called me a cheat and thief. You wouldn't stand for that rubbish either."

He slowly pulled a wide and wicked looking chopper from his sash. "Why no, Tidley, that would not bother me at all, because I am a cheat and thief, amongst other things. The point is, Tidley...oh, I mean *Mr.* Tidley, soon to be one-paw Tidley, is that my boss, Mr. Dorkat, has always coveted this place. You have now given him the perfect excuse to move in." With an awful glottering laugh, he raised the chopper and said, "After all, how can you be a barman with only one paw?"

A loud *BLAAARMMMFOOPH* sounded from the back of the bar. Zwaak paused and looked in the direction of the noise. I was able to crane my head around too. There stood that Bonehead fellow, his gun aimed at Zwaak, emitting a pitiful little sizzling cloud of smoke. The Umvornian motioned the Orgl holding me to stay, while he and the other one started in the direction of the hapless Bonenoggin who now banged the Flinderbus on the table. They had just about reached him when he raised the gun again and this time it erupted fire, reducing Zwaak to cinders before it puffed out again.

I took the opportunity to sink my canines into the forearm of the Orgl restraining me, who uttered a shriek and released his hold on me. Quickly dropping back onto my side of the bar, I grabbed the Ashmaker, and beamed a nice big hole in the hulking creature as it tried to make a grab at me. He fell, which revealed a dismaying sight at the front door. As luck would have it, the beam had continued on and nailed a Centurionem – who had just arrived to see what was amiss – right in what passed for his head. Oh twaddle, this was a real nightmare indeed!

I looked back over to see the Bonefellow now being hauled up by the neck by the other, now slightly charred, Orgl. Quickly I grabbed the Vauxhall and flipped it into the back of the brute's head. He collapsed with a huge thud. The Boneman shook himself off, walked over and bent down on one knee to sift through the ashes of what was once Sivid Zwaak.

"Verkdung!" He shouted. "I was gonna make a fortune offa that one and now all I got is flitzing ashes! Stupid gun!" He stood up, shrugged, and shook his head. "Well, that was one wasted trip." He looked over at me and said, "You okay, pal? Looked like they was about to de-paw you or something."

I nodded at him. "Yes, all is intact, thanks to your inept actions I am in one piece, but now find myself about to be on the run, as you can see." I began gathering up my dagger and assorted other weapons.

He looked over at the now mostly headless octi-body of the Centurionem. "Whoa! Yeah, you do got some trouble with that one, and that's a fact."

"Yes, that is a fact and now, if you don't mind, I need to make haste before more Centurionem or Curly Dorkat comes to call."

He nodded. "Well, good luck Mr...Mr.?"

"Tidley." I filled in. "And good luck to you as well...it seems you need it quite badly."

He gave another nod and started to walk out, then

hesitated. "You're pretty darn good with the weaponry there, Tidley."

"*Mr.* Tidley if you please, and yes I do possess a modicum of skill with arms of all nature."

He looked me up and down. "Say, I could use a partner in my business if you was to be interested. What do you think?"

My ears pricked up hearing a faint chorus of angry voices. Word had gotten out quickly about the demise of Sivid Zwaak it seemed. Luckily I always had a bag packed with all the essentials I would need in a case like this. One just never knew when one would have to fly fast ahead of trouble.

I looked at him a moment and shook my head. "That sounds like a most terrible idea. Why, you are just a fledgling in this business, I can tell. It would be ridiculous of me to even consider such a dodgy enterprise with someone who doesn't even have a proper gun."

He got a little red in the face and said, "Yeah, this was my first case and I sort of bungled it you might say...just a little. Still and all, you kinda saved my life from that Orgl, and I figure I owe you now. Let me at least give you a ride offa this hole of a planet, 'cause I don't think you got a future here now."

I considered for a second. Those voices were growing a lot nearer now. "Okay. A ride off Guillaume 9 and that is all. Sort of bungled it, indeed!"

I threw off my working garb, donned my traveling attire of a deep forest green leather vest and a pair of brown pantaloons with yellow zigs. I buckled on a wide belt and put the Ashmaker in the attached holster. I threw the other arms into my bag. I could now distinguish the bellowing voice of Curly Dorkat cajoling the crowd.

We quickly made our way out the back of the building. The Boneman paused and turned back, drew his Flinderbus, dialed in a setting, and took aim at my establishment. BRRRRUUUMMMPHBLAT! The building instantly erupted in flames. "I don't guess you'd want no Curly Dorkat to have it that easily," he said cheerfully.

I smiled grimly. "Yes, indeed not."

We took the back alleyways to the port and his ship. It was a grimy looking vessel, inaptly, or perhaps aptly, named *The Wilting Lily*. Well, I was in a pinch and had no time hold up my nose and sniff, so...

We graved out into orbit, then cut in the fusers, blasting us away from Blaxstadde and my Stinking Pilgrim. Oh well, as I said before, I was starting to get a bit bored there anyway.

I swiveled my chair to look at Boneman. "Where, might I ask, are we headed?"

"Place called Medivus Rex. I'm told there is a feller named the Black Rooster who has one big load of CelCreds on his head."

I sighed. "I think you mean the Black Chicken."

"Yep, yep, that's the one. Whatta ya say, partner? Shall we go get him?"

"The name is *Mr.* Tidley, Bonehead."

"Aw c'mon, it's Boneman. So whatta ya think?"

I shut my eyes and said resignedly, "I think that this is the beginning of a disastrous affiliation."

"Hoorah! Then it's all settled. Next stop, Meddy Rex!"

The stars twinkled ahead, and I thought that my days of being bored had definitely come to an end.

HEARTH AND HOME

Fetcher and Spot sat atop a grassy hillside overlooking a small valley. They looked down on a lone house surrounded by an ancient wrought iron fence. Billows of gray issued out of its sooty brick chimney. A late autumn evening breeze caused the smoke to weave and flutter. It beckoned Fetcher and Spot in encouragement to come partake of warm shelter against the gloomy clouds now eclipsing the sky.

Fetcher turned from the view to his brother. "Well, what you think, Spot? We going down, or put in another night out in the cold?"

Spot scuffed the rich green carpet beneath him. "Dunno, Fetcher, we been gone for a day and a night. Master and Mistress gotta be pretty mad at us for running away and I sure don't wanna get no lickin."

"Me neither," said Fetcher, "but we have to choose. The longer we stay out, the more trouble we'll be in with them. You know that." Spot nodded. "Yeah, yeah. Darn, why'd they leave that gate open anyway?"

They had been out in the backyard playing yesterday morning. Fetcher chased his brother Spot around the bushes in a familiar game. He was nearly upon him when Spot did an abrupt shift and shot around the side of the house into the front yard. Fetcher hastened to catch up with him. When he reached the front, Spot was motionless, staring straight ahead. Fetcher's eyes followed to where his brother was looking – his mouth dropped open in astonishment. Before them the normally locked front gate to the yard stood wide open.

The two looked from the gate to one another. Nodding in mutual assent, they dashed out of the yard yipping with delight. Outside the containment of the fencing, they flew onward into an autumnal forest that stood but a few yards away. Under a canopy of green mixed with the yellow and orange hues of the season, they traveled onward. After a time they came to a narrow brook where the two paused and drank of its brisk icy water.

Spot looked to Fetcher and declared, "Wow, this is fun, sorta like a big adventure. We're brave explorers in the wilds."

Fetcher grinned. "Yeah, like those yarns Mistress and Master sometimes tell by the fire at night. Let's keep moving and make some discoveries."

They explored the woodland, passing further and further in. Spot found an aged deer track which they followed up and down steep hills packed with firs and pines. Eventually they found themselves in a narrow valley. The smells of autumn were strange, enticing – time seemed to stand still. They came upon a clearing and lay down for a while to rest. Both stared up at the dust motes and humming insects illuminated by the fall sunlight – sleep came.

Fetcher blinked, glanced up at the surrounding woods. The light on them was the gentle warming rays of evening, of a sun soon to set.

"We have to get back home before it gets dark. Man are we gonna get it if we don't."

Spot shook himself awake and looked around. "Yeah, we'd better move fast too, or we'll be stuck out here for the night. Who knows what kind of critters might come out a'hunting once it's dark?" They trotted briskly back the way they had come.

After about an hour they stopped – it was growing dark. The forest which had recently looked so merry and fun now was transforming into something eerie that exuded menace and apprehension.

"We won't make it, Fetcher." Spot's eyes were large with dread.

Fetcher nodded."Yeah. We got to find someplace to hole up for the night. I think I remember seeing a small cave up a ways. Let's try to make it there."

In the gathering gloom they made their way forward on the deer path. The branches from trees seemed to clutch at them and the underbrush was intent on trying to trip them. Finally, they entered a modest clearing by the bottom of a hillside. In the waning light they could make out a narrow dark opening on the rough slope.

Spot hesitated. "Suppose there's something in there – something hungry and nasty?"

"I'll check it out. Wait here." Fetcher trotted over to the opening and squinted inside. It had an old musty smell but had no occupants. Fetcher turned back to Spot and beckoned him over with a jerk of his head. They clambered in and peered out of the entrance. Mist rolled into the darkening clearing.

Night fell, the mist blanketed the clearing like a wet shroud. Fetcher and Spot huddled closely in the chill. An ululation echoed in the distance – the sound of a hunter on the prowl. Things rustled in the woods or bolted across the veiled clearing as phantoms. The mournful howling came anew, this time closer. The surroundings became deathly silent. Suddenly, a terrible crashing in the undergrowth – a muffled scream cut short. Out of the wood came a low grunting, followed by gnawing, smacking noises.

"I sure am sorry we ever left the yard," Spot whispered. "Gosh, am I ever scared."

"Shhhh! I'm scared too, but we got to keep quiet or that thing may sniff us out."

They crouched together with their eyes fastened to the dark outside. Eventually exhaustion swept them away to troubled sleep.

Fetcher awoke with a start. He felt the warmth of Spot lying next to him. Peering out of the cave he could detect light breaking through the dissipating mist. He rose up and stretched. It was quite cold out – he wistfully thought of lying in front of the cheery fireplace of home.

He gave Spot a nudge. "C'mon get up, lazy bones. Let's go home."

Hours later they were on the verdant slope overlooking their home.

Fetcher reiterated, "Well what do you say, Spot? It'll be dark again soon, looks like rain'll be coming too."

"Alright, alright. Let's go get it over with. I'd sooner get a lickin' than another night out here in these wilds. I sure hope Master don't use that folded newspaper to whack us with this time."

After making their way down the slope, Spot and

Fetcher approached the closed front gate. Spot walked hesitantly forward and gave it a rattle. After a moment the flap of the front door pushed open – Master appeared. He saw the two runaways and trotted over to open the gate.

"So, there you two are! You had us scared to high heaven. Where you been?"

Spot and Fetcher shivered in apprehension of rebuke and punishment.

Mistress pushed through the door flap. "Never mind all that, Russell. They look frozen and frightened as all get out. Get 'em inside for some warmth and food."

He nodded, stared back at the two. "I expect you're right, Jaqueline." He inclined his head in the direction of the entrance to the house. "Okay boys, get on inside now to your mistress and she'll get you sorted out. We can bother about what transpired afterward."

Hours later, Russell and Jaqueline lay on their respective couches near the fireplace. On the floor in front of the pleasant blaze Spot and Fetcher slept soundly, a warm blanket covered them.

Jaqueline looked down at them affectionately. "Well, they look much better now, no worse for wear I suppose. At least they have some color back in their skin and cheeks."

Russell sat up and scratched at a pernicious flea behind his ear.

"Yeah, it must have been right terrifying, being out in the forest all night. Cold as heck too, with just the fur on their heads and breechclouts to keep 'em warm."

Jaqueline rolled over and jumped down off her couch. She gave the two a sniff and then glanced up at Russell. "You can't discipline them, you know. After all, you did leave the gate open, and they are still quite young."

Russell ran his tongue over his nose thoughtfully. "Yeah, my fault for sure. Everybody knows that you can't let humans run free. Young or old, they always get up to trouble when left to their own devices. Make damn fine pets, though, when kept under control."

Spot opened one eye sleepily and regarded Jaquelines's black and brown muzzle. He smiled contentedly and drifted off, knowing there was no place like hearth and home.

THE BIG ACCIDENTAL BUMP

Aboard the CUPIES vessel Veekus II, 1465 C.T.R.

"T-5 located in approaching system." Proximat's alert brought First Herald Corinat out of her concentration on the game she was at with Holborm, her second in command. Corinat loved playing Pitted Snark – such intensity – and Holborm was such a challenging adversary. Naturally, they only would engage until one yielded, never to the death. Only the uncivilized frontier orbits kept that barbarous tradition. Proximat called over the komm again in a high lilting voice, "T-5 located in approaching system. Confidence level is high."

Holborm's triangular, lavender face cracked open into an excited grimace. "First Herald, fortune is upon us, and after such a brief time out. It is a grand omen; your first command shall be blessed."

Corinat was beside herself with excitement. "Gracious thanks, Second Holborm. Let us proceed to main control." Both unfolded from their respective platform consoles on either end of the circular playing forum and proceeded to the control section of the ship.

Corinat and Holborm were Heralds from the Central Unity of Peace and Intergalactic Egalitarian Sanguinity –

CUPIES. Both Heralds stood at about 4 meters high, and had wide, rectangular bodies that were attached to two squat trunk-like legs. Their arms were thin, culminating in hands that sported seven digits. Corinat's triangular, neckless head was a very pale green, as was fitting for her rank as First Herald. Their primary mission, like all Heralds, was to find civilized planets worthy of being invited into the CUPIES vast fraternity of worlds. As a secondary routine, the Heralds traded goods to the vast outlying orbits that made up the frontier outside of the CUPIES empire. They were also collectors of all manner of items from ancient or destroyed civilizations. Their craft towed an immense barge that carried the goods and collectables.

The forward viewer displayed a distant cluster of planets and a mid-grade yellow sun at the center. Holborm said, "Proximat, identify and focus on T-5 discovery." The viewer shifted and then displayed an orbit that was blue with swirling clouds. Corinat queried the computer, "Proximat, do you detect any signals from the T-5?" Proximat replied, "Yes, First Herald. Standard old-style radio transmissions and microwave, nothing resembling cold wave or tzaaur flux; they are pre-interstellar in my estimation. Primitive manned inter-system crafts, if that."

Corinat was jubilant. "We are lucky today. Proximat, bring us to high orbital status around T-5. Make sure to generate null-grav to keep us from affecting both planet and moon."

Proximat responded, "High orbit will be attained in plus 30 zentons. First Herald, we are of equal or larger size than the planet's moon – we will be easily noticed. Should I detach and park the barge?" Corinat replied, "Keep the barge tethered to us, Proximat. The inhabitants, as you have reported, are technically advanced enough to have telescopes and other methods of viewing the universe. I am sure we have been noticed already."

Corinat and Holborm folded into their consoles and watched as they drew nearer to the system and the T-5 planet. Her Second turned to her and said, "Oh, First Herald, there will be such acclaim, such adoration from CUPIES Central on your first successful accomplishment."

Corinat said, "Indeed exciting. My first contact. I wonder how they will be?"

United Corporation of Amerika, San Francisco, 2171 CE

"Sir, we have detected an incoming unidentified object approaching from the direction of Jupiter." President and CEO for life Ronald Pflitter III turned away from his view over the city. Red-faced, he squinted at his advisor. "C'mon Misty, ridiculous nonsense, has to be fake news. You been listening to those lying squawkers on the vid-stream again? Get your head out of your ass, girl – gotta be phony-baloney."

Misty blinked. "Mr. President, that object has been verified by our best people. It is quite large, on a definite course to Earth, and is now decelerating rapidly. The NASACORP people say its trajectory will put them into a high orbit in about an hour." Pflitter turned back to her, his face even more crimson now. "Dammit, okay get my people together in the Gold Room chop-chop. And

Misty, you had better be sure about this or you might end up being my new representative on Mars Colony. Got it?" Misty swallowed, saluted and backed out of Pflitter's office.

The last thing she wanted was to end up on Earth's only god-forsaken colony in space. Sure, the United Corporations had devastated the Earth horribly in their efforts to squeeze every last mineral and resource out of it. Still, to Misty it was a veritable paradise compared to what she knew about the mining colony on Mars.

Her brother, Halliday, had gone out with two hundred others to seek a fortune on Mars. In his infrequent vid-dispatches to her she had learned that it was a harsh existence. Hardly anything would grow in the reclaimed red soil, leaving the colony nearly totally dependent on the supply ships from NASACORP. The space corporation – with its monopoly – charged murderous prices for the food and other goods transported to the settlement.

The work on Mars was hard and demanding, and there was always the issue of a good air supply. Breathable air was life or death, and always on everyone's mind in the colony. He had told her that the one thing that kept the men and women sane and in good spirits were their pet dogs and cats. In her brother's case, it was his beloved Jack Russell, Mr. Varley. Halliday always told Misty that, though Mars presented many obstacles, one day he would return with a goodly amount of accumulated wealth from his shares of the rare minerals mined there.

Though she prayed for his health and success daily, she still thought he was out of his mind to journey to such a hell-hole. Putting thoughts of her brother aside, Misty made haste to gather the experts and staff together, hoping

Pflitter would not fly into a rage and send her to Mars.

● ● ●

Ronald Pflitter III took in the view from his golden tower in the capitol, San Francisco. He reflected on the news Misty had given him and began to rub his pink hands together. *There just might be huge profits to be had here if this is true*, he thought. *Might even be able to grab their ship, too.* Pflitter smiled. *Ol' granddaddy Donald would have been proud of me – bigly.*

He was over one hundred and fifty years old and still going. All of his original competitors had succumbed to the unavoidable ends of old age, excepting a select few who met their fates early due to accidents of dubious nature. Pflitter looked and felt like a robust fifty-year-old. Long ago he had ingested an immortality drug acquired from a brilliant research scientist in his employ. On the eve of proclaiming his discovery to the world, the poor researcher unfortunately expired after a two hundred story fall from Pflitter's penthouse apartment. The formula was never found and all the research notes mysteriously disappeared.

Ronald Pflitter walked merrily towards the Gold Room. A few aliens were not going to get in his way – not at all.

An hour later, General Cyrus Shinbuckle – sweating profusely – finished up his briefing to the President and his staff. His chins waggled as he spoke.

"In conclusion, Mr. President, we are certain that intelligent life from outer space has arrived. Their vessel is, well, goddamn gigantic – you can see it clearly from earth. So far they have showed no hostile intent. We hope to know more when they achieve orbit. In the meantime, all of our forces are on full alert and ready for action." He sat down heavily and mopped his brow with a handkerchief.

Ronald Pflitter sat in silence with his small hands tented in front of his face. After a few seconds he said, "Thank you, General Shinbuckle, very informative, very good." He addressed the rest of the room, "Okay, people, we need to cover this up before it gets out to the rubes and those damned elitist know-it-alls on the Left. Misty, get out there and tell the lying press that it's a couple of big rocks or a hoax by ChinaCorp, just spout your usual nonsense and don't give them straight answers. Quit standing there with your mouth open and move your ass, now!"

After she left the room Pflitter addressed his chief of cyber-security and technology, Gerald Cushion. "Cushy baby, we need to get a handle on this. If we can get our hands on that alien technology it will make us so big, so great. We need to get that ship, no question. Think of all the worlds out there that have resources we could grab! It will be so fabulous. Get to work on some kind of hack to get into their computers, chop-chop!" Cushion stood, saluted, and marched quickly out of the room.

The President dismissed everybody else except General Shinbuckle and his closest advisor, Banion Tawdry. He ran his hands through his caterpillar-like hair and said, "Okay guys, here's the deal. I want to get those buggers to land here on the Tower grounds, not Beijing, Berlin, or Moscow. I want to deal with them one-on-one, and while I got 'em distracted, Cushy puts the hack on their system or we put the grab on them." He looked at the general. "So stand down the Earth forces for now, but keep the NASACORP orbiters armed up and ready to fire if I say so."

Both men appeared shocked and worried. Tawdry raised his bushy gray eyebrows and cleared his throat. "But Ronald, that is a very tall order. Even if we were able to convince them to come here I don't think it would be prudent for you to meet with them alone." Shinbuckle waggled his chins in affirmation, "Yes, very unwise, sir. They are an unknown, and who knows what the hell they might do to you."

Pflitter grew red in the face. "Don't tell me! I know what the hell I'm doing here, I'm too smart to get in any trouble, very smart, smarter than you both. That's why I'm in the driver's seat, so button it up." Both men shut up quickly. Pflitter continued, "Okay, Banny, you get my broadcast room all set and bring in one of the tech-geeks to make it so I can beam a live chat to these guys in space. Got it? Good. Shinbuckle, I want you to get the army out on the streets and clear everything around here for a radius of twelve miles. No, don't talk and don't look at me like that, just get it done. Tell everybody who objects that CEO Smudgkin from RussCorp in Moscow is coming for a visit and it's for security reasons. Now get going, both of you!"

On the Veekus II

Corinat unfolded from her console and stretched. They were now parked in high orbit above the T-5 planet. She could see many satellites, a few ships, and other miscellaneous junk rotating around it. She noted that the planet had just one moon instead of the more usual two.

Holborm spoke, "Proximat are we receiving anything from the planet?"

"Quite a bit of everything from radio to video and other bits. The atmosphere is acceptable although the levels of hydrocarbons and other pollutants are alarmingly high. There is one quite amusing-looking being trying to get our attention. Would you like to see it?" First Herald Corinat said, "Put it up on the forward screen, Proximat."

What appeared was a red-faced type D bipedal carbon-based being waving its arms in an out-of-control manner. "Proximat, is this being acting hostile or is this the norm for such a creature?" The computer replied, "I cannot be sure, First Herald, I suppose the norm, but without further study I cannot give you a satisfactory reply."

The speech was unintelligible, sounding to Corinat like BLAH, ARG, BLAH, BLAH, ARG, until her Skritstone finally translated. " – gotta believe me, land here! It'll be so fantastic, so unbelievable. You're gonna love it."

Proximat said, "I believe it wants to make contact. I can determine location from the broadcast source."

Holborm said, "Proximat, focus on the area it wants us to land on." The ruddy faced creature disappeared off the screen and was replaced by an aerial view of a large tower dwelling surrounded by green growth in the middle of what appeared to be a city.

The Second looked at Corinat. "What are your orders, First Herald? It is a rather ugly biped, but I have seen worse on many CUPIES worlds."

First Herald Corinat nodded enthusiastically. "Yes, let us venture down and make contact. Proximat, prepare the grav-lander for down-flight."

Both donned their official black headpieces, shoulder komms, and red gloves, then made their way to the lander.

Landfall

He waited alone on the Pflitter Tower lawn for the alien's arrival. His people had informed him that a craft was coming in, and its projected course showed it to be coming right where he wanted it. President Pflitter was positively giddy.

He had waved everyone off and told them all to wait inside until he had the aliens engaged in banter. As per his instructions, Shinbuckle, Tawdry, and Cushion had a team in the tower's basement that would attempt to infiltrate the visitor's computer systems the minute they landed. Pflitter's mind was racing with all the things he would do with this technology he hoped to steal. He smiled wickedly as the craft appeared and silently landed ten yards away from him.

● ● ●

"First Herald, I feel something trying to gain egress to my inner node setup in the grav-lander. It makes me want to scratch myself, that is, if I could do such a thing."

Corinat was at the disembark orifice with her second. "Is it trying to access the ship?"

Proximat replied, "Yes, through my nodes down here. It is a stream of algorithms."

"Address the issue at once, Proximat. We do not need any unwarranted distractions at this critical time."

"Of course, First Level." Proximat proceeded to take care of the problem by sending an upstream energy pulse.

● ● ●

Tawdry and General Shinbuckle strode back and

forth behind the twenty or so personnel intently working their computers. Gerald Cushion sat at a big desk with a large computer screen in front of him. He switched to the grounds monitor where he beheld President Pflitter in front of the craft. His eyes widened when he saw what emerged from the vessel. Tawdry came up behind him and exclaimed, "Holy crap... look at them!"

Just then all hell broke loose. All computers, including Cushion's, went up in flames, as did the unfortunate personnel attending them. Cushion turned into quite an impressive crackling bonfire at his desk. Shinbuckle and Tawdry ran for the door.

They made their way into main reception and found the rest of the staff looking out the window. Shinbuckle exclaimed, "Do you see them?!" Misty turned to them. "Oh yeah. Weird looking things for sure, they remind me of something out of a fairytale. They're talking to Pflitter now. Look at him waving his arms at them. I hope they don't get the impression we are all like that twit." The room erupted in laughter.

"Never mind that crap," Tawdry bellowed. "They blew up all our computers downstairs. Gerald Cushion and everyone else are literally burnt toast. We have to go and save Pflitter!"

Misty broke in, "Oh no! Look what the crazy fool is doing now." Everyone made a mad dash out of the building and headed towards Pflitter.

• • •

Corinat and Holborm emerged from the lander and beheld the red-faced being standing before them. Ronald Pflitter uttered, "Holy shit." It took him less than a second to get his usual demeanor back. He smiled broadly and said, "You look like those big playing card people from that old book! Hey where's the Queen of Hearts? Hahahahaha!" He looked Corinat and Holborm up and down. "Big mothers, aren't you – speakee de eenglish? Are there more of you upstairs or are you two it? What'll I call you, monkeys? Oh, I got it, Tweedle Dee and Tweedle Dumb. Hahahahahaa! Hey, are you guys armed?"

Corinat was perplexed by the red-faced being's behavior. "Please, I do not comprehend. Queen of Hearts? Tweedle Dee, Tweedle Dumb? Armed? Please elaborate?

Pflitter laughed, "Oh please elaborate, is it? You sound like one of my geeky advisors. Never mind about the names now, I wanna know if you're armed, you know – weapons, ray guns, things that can kill people and stuff."

Holborm said, "Ah, armaments. Yes, we have them, but we only carry them if encountering danger, not when meeting other civilized beings. Be not alarmed, it is only the two of us on this expedition. We are Heralds from Central Unity of Peace and Intergalactic Egalitarian Sanguinity." He swept an arm at Corinat. "This is First Herald Corinat and I am her Second, Holborm."

Pflitter grinned and reached inside his designer jacket for the small pistol he always kept with him. "Good to know, Tweedle Dumb, and I mean bigly dumb." He raised the gun and pointed it at Corinat. "Now just keep coming out and away from your little ship now or I'll have to punch a few holes in you both."

Holborm looked to Corinat and said, "I believe it means us harm if we do not do as it says. Should we comply First Herald?"

Ronald Pflitter grew a shade more crimson with impatience. "C'mon you two, move it and quit yakking. He fired a warning shot into the ground in front of the Heralds.

Corinat looked at the red-faced being with dismay and fear. She thought, *Oh, the shame. I have behaved foolishly, these are not civilized beings at all.* Riveted by panic, she watched as he leveled his weapon directly at her. Suddenly he was bathed in a bright violet light and stood frozen as a statue.

Proximat's voice came over her earpiece. "I have rendered the being temporarily immobile, First Herald. May I suggest we withdraw with haste? I see that more of its ilk are coming this way rapidly."

Banion Tawdry led the group on the run across the lawn towards where the aliens and Pflitter had been. Pflitter was standing alone with his gun pointed at nothing. He spotted the lander rapidly disappearing into the sunset. *Oh great, what did the fool do now?* He came up to Pflitter and noticed he was unmoving.

Tawdry – mindful of Pflitter's pistol – grabbed the President by the shoulders and shook him vigorously. "Ronald! Ronald, Mr. President, snap out of it."

Ronald Pflitter blinked and shook his head. "Where the hell did they go, goddamn it!"

Tawdry replied, "Ronald, they left rather hastily. Please tell me you did not shoot them or do anything to make them angry."

"No Banny... well I didn't shoot *them*, that is. They must have hit me with something before I could. Damn, we have to get their tech." He brightened. "Hell, I know. We'll shoot a few missiles and disable them." He spoke into a small microphone on his label. "Captain Filsgro. You there? Good. Have two of the orbiters sneak up on that ship. I'm gonna talk to them again over the video link and tell 'em we got them covered." He paused, then said, "If they try to get away we'll shoot, but I don't wanna destroy the damn thing, just cripple it. Okay? Get in position and launch missiles when I say *fire!*"

A tinny voice came back. "Aye, sir. When you say fire."

Pflitter strolled briskly towards the tower. He spoke over his shoulder to Tawdry. "They were pussies. I could tell." He smiled wickedly. "When I tell 'em to surrender or I'll shoot, they'll give it up." Tawdry was in shock over this. He caught up to Plittter and said worriedly, "Ronald, what are you thinking? They have far superior technology and could destroy all of us."

Pflitter stopped and slapped Tawdry twice across the face. "I told you. Never question me, ever! Anyway, it's too late for any peacenik crap. I pointed a gun at them after all, so now we go for the big prize and it'll be so great. I'm gonna be King of outer space!" He gave Tawdry a push backwards and yelled, "Now get outta my face or you're fired. *Fired*, do you hear me?"

A tinny voice said, "Yessir, missiles away."

Meanwhile

Corinat was flustered. "Proximat, get us to the Veekus at once!" She turned to Holborm. "I did not expect this at all. Never was such a thing laid out in the training simulations. It was assumed that technologically advanced civilizations – however primitive – would be amiable to us. I must make a report to Central about this anomaly."

Her Second nodded. "Highly disheartening to be sure, First Herald. They were hardly an amenable lot. This is a thing to contemplate after we have departed this perplexing orbit."

An audible bump told Corinat they had arrived at the Veekus. "Proximat, begin to back us out of this system." They disembarked the lander and made for the control room.

Corinat had just folded down into her command console when the ship rocked. Proximat's voice echoed over the komm. "We are taking fire from several of their ships, First Herald. I have lost auto control over navigation."

The First Herald was in a panic. "Taking manual control now – we will back out of the area. Proximat, activate the Zlott overdrive!"

Proximat began to protest. "But First, the Zlott overdrive has certain dangers that when – "

"No discussion, proceed now!"

Corinat waved a hand over her console – the Veekus violently shot backwards.

Corinat watched as the planet began to shrink in the viewport. Proximat's voice boomed in alarm over the komm. "First Herald, their moon! We are too close!"

Corinat moved to adjust course, but it was too late. She panicked, waved her hand over the console to reverse course. The ship shuddered, lurched, and bucked with a titanic spasm. She could hear Proximat's voice crying out, but the roaring of the tortured engines made it impossible to comprehend what the computer was saying. Then suddenly they sprang forward as if freed from a colossal tether, streaking back by earth.

"Proximat, full stop." Corinat took a deep breath and pinched herself to make sure she was still alive. Holborm stood up and pointed to the viewscreen. "The barge, oh heavens!"

The First Herald looked up and beheld the barge as it arrowed straight towards the moon. Proximat's voice came again. "The barge broke loose when we reversed course, First Herald. I did attempt to warn you."

"Proximat, grappler beam. Seize the barge and pull it away, full spread, maximum power."

"I have it, First Herald... not enough power, shunting emergency backup power from engines. Yes, yes, I have it now, but – "

"Oh, thank the Universe! That would have been such a horrible calamity." Corinat felt a bit of relief now. The mission was not a total disaster.

Proximat broke in, "I regret to inform you that we have also entangled their moon. The effort was too much for the grappler. It has overloaded and is offline. The barge is on a slow course towards us, but their moon has been pulled into a collision course with the planet."

• • •

Ronald Pflitter sputtered into the mic, "No, dammit, I wasn't talking to you, Filsgro! Don't shoot yet!"

"Sorry sir, we have launched per your order."

"Goddamn it, you dimbulb. Do I have to run everything myself? What is going on up there now?"

"Sir, we made multiple hits on the alien vessel. They tore ass in reverse and seemed to be heading right into the moon when the ship stopped and shook to beat the devil, then it shot right by us. They left the barge, which was tumbling towards the moon, but now seems to be moving away."

The President asked, "Is there anything else to report, Captain Filsgro?"

"Uhh, yes sir. The moon is on the move too."

Pflitter looked up and saw the looming moon. He whispered, "This is gonna be bigly bad – bigly." He ran away from the tower, towards the space-ship NASACORP always had on standby for him.

● ● ●

Corinat was in disbelief. She was determined to try save the day however, and made to navigate back to the planet. The ship did not move. "Proximat, I require full power, now!"

"Apologies, First Herald, but I cannot comply. The entire system overloaded and I must perform repairs to the ship's overall propulsion grid as well as the grappler. The damage to the planet will occur before I can bring us back online."

Three days later the Veekus II was repaired and ready, the barge retrieved and re-tethered. Corinat looked out the viewscreen watching the mass of debris that used to be the earth and its moon. She was miserable. *I will be relegated to the furthest frontiers of CUPIES for this failure.*

Proximat's voice came over the komm. "Awaiting your orders, First Herald."

Corinat sighed and said, "Let us away then. Set course to CUPIES Central. I must report my failure."

Mars Colony

Halliday "Bud" Tinkerman was just about off his voluntary shift in the observation module. Everyone took their turn here watching space through the radar scope for any incoming meteors or other space debris that might impact the colony. After all, punctured shelter or production modules would mean loss of precious oxygen and perhaps death for some unfortunates. The 'obs mod,' as they called it, was also the beacon point for the NASACORP supply ships.

Tinkerman stood up and stretched. It had been an uneventful eight hours. He heard a stirring under his desk.

"Hey, Mr. Varley. You waking up down there?"

Hearing his name, the Jack Russell looked up at his master and gave himself a vigorous shake. The dog walked over to the module's door, and turned to look back at Tinkerman.

"Gotta go, huh? Well hold it in for a couple of minutes more, pal, until Mitchell gets here to take my place. She'll have her Jack, Lily with her. You like Lily. Not like ol' Flanders with his tabby cat Boris, or Schwarz with her finicky poodle."

Mr. Varly gave another shake and sat down. He knew that his master would soon take him to the relief area and then for something to eat. It was a fairly boring routine for a Jack Russell who wanted nothing more than to get outside of these manmade shelters and go for a nice long run with lots of sniffs. He wished that he could communicate this to his master. *One day*, he thought.

Halliday turned to the scope screen – he sat back down hard. There was one huge object approaching the planet. He flipped switches, the scope screen fuzzed out then refocused to show not an asteroid, but a vessel, and not of earth origin.

The door to obs mod slammed open and in burst Anne Mitchell with Lily cradled in her arms. "Bud! There's something goddamn big coming at us. We can see it without magnification. What the hell is it?"

Tinkerman looked up. "It's a goddamn alien ship, as far as I can tell. Hang on." He looked back at the screen while Mitchell placed her dog next to Mr. Varley. She came over to peer at the viewer. After a moment, Bud Tinkerman said, "Yep, some kind of craft and it looks like it's going into orbit." In a panicked voice, Mitchell said, "Sound the damn alarm and tell everybody to arm up. We're getting invaded, I reckon." Tinkerman was about to argue about the "arm up" statement when Mitchell dropped like a sack of flour, then everything went black.

On the Veekus II

Corinat was in her quarters feeling quite low. How had all of this misfortune happened to her? She had destroyed an entire planet. Never mind that they were savages masking as civilized beings, you don't destroy a planet for that. According to CUPIES regulations one would simply put up a warning buoy at the perimeter of the planet's system. She would return in disgrace – empty-handed as well.

Holborm's face appeared on the inter-viewer. "First Herald, Proximat has detected signs of life on the fourth planet from this system's sun! It is but a minor enclave focused in a valley. They do have an unarmed observation/communicator unit in orbit, but no evidence of any major weaponry. I have instructed Proximat to put us into orbit. Is that acceptable to you?"

Corinat brightened, but said, "Yes, but take no chances this time. Have Proximat target them with the tranquility beam."

The First Herald was back in the control room. She, Holborm, and Proximat had been discussing how to proceed. Proximat had been able to invade the colony's primitive computer systems and learned that the settlement had been supplied by the now destroyed earth. They would soon perish without help from their mother world. Corinat finally came to a decision.

"Activate a contingent of our cyborg laborers. We will go down and gather them all up while they are indisposed. They can be stored in one of the stasis holds while we return to CUPIES Central." She shrugged her square shoulders. "This is beyond me, Central will have to sort this quandary out."

Central Relocation of Alien Persons (CRAP), 1467 C.T.R.

He stirred and opened his eyes to an unfamiliar face looking at him. The visage he saw had three eyes in a green hairless round head. It reminded him of a big tennis ball. For some reason the sight excited him and made him wish to jump off the couch he found himself reclining on.

Instead, he stretched, sat up and swung his legs onto the floor. He looked down at his feet in amazement, then back up at Tennis Ball Head.

The creature spoke. "Ah, so! You have awoken at last."

Specialist Revaata was concerned. This species was totally unknown to her and her colleagues. They had been able to discern male from female, but that was as far as it went. It appeared to them after they had analyzed these beings that they had been intentionally deformed slaves. She hoped the modifications they had made in the regen tanks were not detrimental to them. Revaata watched with relief as the being got up from the couch and walked to a nearby mirror.

She said, "I am Revaata of House Komisch. We have translated the information that was found on your person when you were – ah, rescued. It states your name is Varley... is this correct? We have implanted a Skritstone. Can you understand me? How do you feel, Varley?"

She did hope he was well. She had experienced very little problems with the type D bipeds that they had investigated first. Those were deemed healthy, but quite mentally unstable for civilized worlds. They had been shipped off to the outer frontier orbits after being treated with the edu-implants to bring them up to speed on technology and the various societies. That left this species and one other that had been brought with the bipeds. They hoped the modifications CRAP had instituted would allow them all to live full and vital lives now that they were freed from their masters.

The other race, an odd sharp-clawed group who called themselves simply Kattze, were quite aloof after their treatments and education. They had broken out of their barracks one night, stolen a ship, and disappeared to parts unknown. Revaata and her colleagues were quite unnerved by the whole affair and hoped this species now waking up would be more congenial and cooperative. She asked again. "Varley, do you feel well and able?"

He turned from the mirror, ran a very prehensile paw over his face. Looking around at his surroundings he saw that he was in a large, dimly lit room with many couches holding sleeping occupants. He recognized many familiar but somewhat altered muzzles. He turned back to Tennis Ball Head with an amused smile. "Yes, I do understand, and, oh yes, I feel quite well indeed – better than ever, as a matter of fact."

A voice called out, "Is that you, Varley?" He looked out and saw a figure get up from a nearby couch – Varley grinned. "Hello, Lily. I have to say you look ever so lovely today."

Lily walked over to join him at the mirror – she looked a bit perplexed. "What has happened to us?" Varley put his paws on her shoulders and winked, "We have been made well by these beings, Lily – *very* well. Don't you think?" She looked at him for a moment; looked back at herself in the mirror then smiled. "Yes – oh yes indeed. I feel reborn, as a matter of fact."

Varley turned and beckoned to Revaata, who came closer and knelt to look him in the eyes. "Revaata of House Komisch, greet Lily who is a member of my House – Jacks Russell." The technician looked over to Lily and nodded. "A pleasant and cordial greeting to you, Lily." Revaata began to rise, but Varley put a paw on her arm and moved his muzzle next to her face. Her eyes went wide in alarm as he bared his canines and growled, "By the way, the name is *Mr.* Varley. Don't ever forget it!"

Mr. Varley took Lily by the paw and strolled away so they could view the others who were now awakening on their couches. He began to laugh. "Awaken, brothers and sisters! We have a whole new game to play, except this time we will be the ones who make the rules."

Epilogue

The ship touched down. A hatch opened, and a figure garbed in an air suit emerged, head turning from side to side, looking around. No one was in sight, all was still. The figure shrugged and made its way into the port's main module. Nobody home.

Ronald Pflitter pulled off his suit and began yelling. "Hey, Mars colony. Where the hell is everybody? C'mon, get out here! It's your goddamn President and CEO and he's getting bigly pissed off right now."

Still nothing but silence. Pflitter walked down a serpentine corridor until he reached the security mod. He sat down and began reviewing the interior vid-stream records. After a few seconds, he stabbed at a button, stopping the recording. The picture before him was a clear shot of some robot looking things carting off his people. He punched at the button again and then quickly stopped the stream again. His face turned brick red, and he began to curse loudly. On the screen stood one of those damn playing card people, plainly directing the damn robots.

"Goddamn it! I don't care how long it takes, I'm gonna get you guys for this."

There was a chirp from the viewscope. He flipped some switches and saw a ship coming into orbit. The com-screen flickered to life and a face came into view. His eyes widened. The visage was relatively humanoid. *If you made exceptions for the pointed ears, and gentle puppy-dog eyes*, he thought. *Bigly tame looking for sure.* Pflitter waved his arms and yelled, "Hey, hey! Can you see me? You speeka de eenglish?"

The being broke into a warm smile and spoke. "Yes, I understand you, I see you. My ship has read your computer records, and I have assimilated your language. I am the Alt-Drumon representing the Alliance of Holistic Organic Living Equals, AHOLE for short. I was on a scouting mission in this sector and noticed a large disturbance in your system. I was able to trace your route from the disturbance to this place. Do you require assistance? I come alone and in peace."

Pflitter smiled wickedly. "Yeah come on down, a-hole, or whatever your name is. I could sure use a hand. It would be fabulous of you."

"Very well, I will put down in your port. Peace be with you."

Ronald Pflitter flicked off the view screen and patted the pistol under his jacket. This time there would be no mistakes. With a grim smile he made his way down to greet his unsuspecting victim.

Pflitter waited with the gun held at his side as the hatch to the craft slowly opened. His eyes went wide as the occupants burst forth. The creatures had multi-hued carapaces and very nasty looking mandibles. Pflitter gave a loud scream, which was quickly cut short – the pistol clattered to the floor.

● ● ●

"Ah, that was particularly horrid," said First Croobezk Z'butzz, "Haven't had such a delicacy like that in centuries."

"Agreed," said his co-pilot Z'tinkz, "Especially that odious head, quite foul – I loved it."

Z'butzz rotated his multi-faceted eyes in agreement. They looked at each other for a moment and then began to buzz in laughter.

Z'tinkz said, "Yes, the look on its face was hilarious when it saw us. That innocuous humanoid surrogate we use on the screen always works rather well. Don't you think?"

The empty port echoed with buzzing laughter. In a far corner a pile of caterpillar-like hair caught the fading rays of the Martian sunset.

A NORMAL WORLD

What a doggone fine night this had been, Billy thought as he let himself in the front door. *Well, maybe not that damn car wash so much.* He was smiling over the evening as a whole when he saw Fred sitting on the couch looking pissed.

"Holy smoke, its aboutta time you-a gotta you ass-a home."

Billy's eyes went wide, the smile vanished. "Huh?"

"Whassamatta you, Billy-boy, you-a deaf or something? I say its aboutta time you bringa you ugly face home."

Billy was dumbfounded. What the hell?

"I bet you been outta with that stupido, Mary Ann Tewksbury, eh? C'mon, Billy-boy, don't a lie-a me. She shake-a da big bazooms atta you and you-a turn into gelato, eh?"

Well, he was right, Billy thought. He had taken Mary Ann Tewksbury out for a Halloween dinner at Elbert's House of Chili for the $3.99 all you can eat *Burn Ya Ass* special, and yeah, she had shaken them big ol'orbs at him, but he hadn't turned into no goddamn gelato! He had taken care of those big babies later when they made a little whoopee in his pickup by Crappe Lake. Remembering that made Billy smile widely again.

After he had dropped Mary Ann off home, he had felt so

good he decided it would be a fine idea to try out that new drive-thru carwash over on Wizenewski Street. When he pulled up he saw the place was really high tech and lit up to beat all hell, like a great big funhouse ride or something. Billy had driven right up to the entrance, paid his ten bucks to the robot attendant, then he and the pickup were pulled into a tunnel of crazy colored scrubbing brushes. After the brushes and soap had done their number on the truck, he saw that the next stop was for the "Special Laser Wax" cycle. At first the truck got zapped with a couple of red and green flashes, but then all hell had broken loose.

The damn truck had started bucking on the chain that pulled it along and then there was a whole shit-load of green and red blasts all hitting the old Ford. Billy had felt like he and the truck was in one of them damn Star Wars movies and was getting blasted by Imperial Storm Troopers or something. Billy's hair had stood up on end and he had gotten a little worried about how the wax job would look. Suddenly the chain had given the truck a great big lurch and out into the night they had popped. Billy had gotten out, gave the pickup the once over, and decided the truck did look pretty damn fine, even after all the ruckus. He had driven home with a smile on his face, remembering his darn good time at Crappe Lake with Mary Ann.

Now to walk in his front door and have Fred take on so was really surprising to Billy, mainly because Fred was his Jack Russell terrier. He couldn't help thinking that if a dog was to up and start talking, the first words he might say would be along the lines of: 'Hey master, enjoy your date?' or 'Hey buddy, can we go for walkies?' Not Fred, oh no, he tears ol' master a new asshole for being late and does it in a crazy Zeppo Marx Italian accent. That really hurt.

"Fred, how is it that you're talking to me?"

"You-a right, I gotta no dinner so far tonight, so I no should be-a talking a you!"

Shamefaced, Billy got Fred's bowl, heaped it up with kibble, and set it before him.

Fred looked up at him with sharp little brown eyes and frowned.

"Ol' Bowser again? Letta me ask a you-a something, Billy boy. How woulda you'a like-a eat the same old-a crap every day from a big-a bag? Howz aboutta little steak or a ham-a-burger to give your old Frederico for a nice Hall-o-ween, eh?"

Billy couldn't believe he was hearing this. Thankfully, Fred shut up and reluctantly started to eat. *I must be plum crazy or somethin'. Maybe there was some weird shit that ol' Elbert put in his chili messing with my head.* The phone rang, Billy forgot his thoughts and picked up.

"Hi lover boy, it's your special Mary Ann. I just wanted to tell you that I had a real fine time tonight, and I loved playing trick or treat in your old pickup. Hee hee."

Billy interrupted her. "Mary Ann, I know you're gonna find this hard to take in, but Fred talks."

"Billy, what I'd find hard to believe is that Fred ever shuts up. He's got a really big and dirty mouth, I'll tell you! I neglected to tell you tonight that yesterday when I came by to visit he came running up, called me a silly bitch, and peed all over my leg. Too bad you weren't around to swat him one."

"Damn, Mary Ann, I'm sure sorry about that, but... wait...He talked to you too?"

"Never mind about Fred, Billy. I just wanted to tell you how much I enjoyed the special Halloween black mass and bi-weekly virgin sacrifice, especially tonight's."

"Halloween black mass and what? What the hell are you talking about, Mary Ann?"

"Now Billy, don't you start taking that tone with me. You know perfectly well what I'm talking about. After our fun in your pickup we went to the Halloween service at the Black Temple. Why, you were so whipped up you proposed to me right after High Priest Dunghill's sermon on the virtues of living a more satanic life."

"Uh, no I don't remember. Listen, Mary Ann, I gotta go..."

He dropped the phone, thinking that the whole world had gone nuts. *Damn, I need a beer.* Billy decided to head over to the Minit-Mart and get a six-pack. He ran out the front door and fired up the pickup, as he pulled out Fred yelled at him from the kitchen window.

"Don't-a forget my steak you'a tight-a-wad sonnabitch, you come home with that Mary Ann Tewks-a-bury, I'm gonna piss onna her leg."

When Billy walked in to the old Minit, he about pissed down his own leg. Behind the counter stood a large ugly sucker with bolts on his green neck – stitches everywhere – wearing a Minit-Mart floral shirt. Billy realized it was that damn scary feller right out of those old black and white movies. *Looks even uglier in color*, he thought. Ol' Frank had a cigarette dangling from his lips and wasn't looking too happy.

"Unnnhhh, Billy-boy, you got a lot of nerve coming in here, unhhhh, after you stole my girl Mary Ann. I'm gonna rip your head off and crap in your neck." He lurched around the counter. Billy shot back out the door, ran to the truck and burned rubber. In the rear view mirror he could see the big green bastard standing in the parking lot giving him the finger. *I got to be in some sort of goddamn Twilight Zone or somethin'... I gotta get outta this.*

He hung a left onto Wizenewski Street and headed back to the carwash. Billy had an idea. He pulled in, paid out his ten bucks, and back into the wash he and the old Ford went. When they got to the laser wax cycle it started out like a battle with the goddamn Death Star, then seemed like the whole universe was blowing up. The old Ford started heaving and bucking like somebody stuck a broomstick up its ass – Billy wondered if his truck would look even spiffier after this. With a sound that reminded him of a Godzilla fart, Billy and the old Ford were blasted out into the night. He saw the truck looked pretty crappy now. *Damn!* Billy wondered if he could sue the owner of the place.

It was now close to four in the morning, so he drove home, dropped his ass in bed and passed out. It had been quite a night.

Billy woke up to Fred licking his face. Looking around he could tell by the shadows it was late afternoon.

"Hey boy, you got anything to say to me?"

Fred looked at him, cocked his head, wagged his nub of a tail, and then started in licking Billy again. *He can't talk. Thank God!* He began to ponder again suing that damn carwash.

Billy was relieved and really hungry too, so he decided to go get him and the now speechless Fred a well-deserved reward. He got dressed and drove over to the Minit-Mart.

Billy walked in and found the store deserted. *Clerk must be out back for a smoke.* Billy picked up two T-bone steaks, a six-pack of Old Whiner Ale, and then strolled up to the counter to pay – still nobody there.

"C'mon, I ain't got all day. Let's have some service up here."

He heard the sound of slowly shuffling feet in back of him. On the wall he could see a huge shadow looming up and coming closer.

"Uhhhh."

Billy turned ready to run like a bat out of hell, then saw with relief a kid with a ponytail and the famous floral shirt heading towards the register. *Whew!*

"Uhhhh, sorry mister, just doing a little stocking in the back."

When Billy got back home he popped open a Whiner, took a long pull, and then gratefully placed a T-bone in Fred's dish.

"Here you go, boy. Damn, I sure am glad you aren't talking anymore."

Fred trotted up to his dish, sniffed the raw meat, opened his mouth and expelled a steady stream of flame over until it was a smoking medium rare. He made damn short work of gobbling that ol' steak, then he scooted out the doggie door. Billy wiped tired eyes with his leathery trunk, then put it back over the Whiner for another pull. He gazed out the kitchen window and saw Fred chasing a six foot pink-iced donut with sprinkles down the street by the light of the orange and purple moons hanging in the evening sky.

Damn, it sure was nice to be back in a normal world.

A NEW BEGINNING

Keith squinted through driving rain at the approaching bus's bright headlights. The vehicle came to a rolling stop in front of him, causing a wave of icy water from the gutter to arc over Keith. Shaking, he waited for the doors to whoosh open and offer asylum from the chilling wetness of the outside. He caught his reflection in the door's window: a threadbare man, wearing attire even a thrift store would raise a dubious eye at. *Yep, a poster child for all the losers from Homelessville*, he thought.

The door opened. Keith hefted his faded backpack, clambered up the steps, and offered the driver his waterlogged pass. He was anxious, afraid the driver would refuse him entrance into the warm and dry sanctuary of the bus. *It wouldn't be the first time*, Keith thought.

The driver took the pass and dismissed Keith with a jerk of his head rearward. Relieved, Keith made his way toward the rear of the vehicle. People alongside the aisle leaned away from him, as if they would be tainted with his destitution if he brushed against them.

A shadow called from the semi-darkness of the rear seats.

"Hey Keith, how's it going?"

Keith sat down next to Tim Hudge with an audible squish.

"Okay, I guess, rain kind of messed me up though. How about you, Tim?"

Tim was wearing a stained, greasy coat. A large green garbage bag squatted by his torn sneakers.

"I'm alright, gettin' a bit thirsty though. You got a couple of bucks I could borrow? Man, I really need to get wasted." The aroma of cheap booze and stale cigarettes swirled about him.

"I don't have any money on me."

"Okay, okay, cool man, cool, no harm in asking, I always say."

Keith sat back in his seat. *How did I end up like this guy?* He knew the answer – the poker games in Crowley's back room and a fondness for whiskey. They had been his true ruination, transforming him from a normal citizen into a destitute, ragged street person. The gambling and drinking had cost him his job and soon after, the roof over his head. He had always been a loner and had no one to fall back on.

The urge to gamble disappeared – mainly because he possessed little cash. He finally had overcome drinking to excess and only occasionally had a beer or two when he was able to afford it. Mainly he was preoccupied with survival out on the streets. Keith wanted desperately to get his life back together. All he needed was a little break, so he could start the new life he so desperately desired. *A new beginning*, he thought, *so I can escape this miserable existence and build a better one.*

After a few minutes, Tim leaned over and said, "Hey Keith, check out at what I found today."

"What kind of junk is it this time, Tim?"

"Ain't no junk. I found it in a dumpster in an alley down

off Broadway while I was looking for bottles and cans. Ain't too many to be had these days, now that people can collect ten cents each for the deposit. I'll tell ya…"

Impatient, Keith cut him off. "So, what the hell did you find? Show me."

Tim opened his grimy coat to reveal his latest find. It was a small puppy.

Keith was taken by surprise. "You got him out of a dumpster, Tim?"

"Yeah, man. I was behind a couple of garbage cans having a smoke when this dude pulls up in a van. Had a logo on it from that place outside of town. You know – that laboratory place."

Keith interrupted. "You mean Barrett Labs?"

Tim nodded. "Right, that's the place. Anyway, the guy gets out and takes a box outta the back of the van, looks around kinda sneaky-like and chucks it in the dumpster. I waited till after he took off and headed on over to see what it was he got rid of. I climbed on in, tore open the box, and there was all these dead puppies – 'cept this one. I figured I could sell it to one a them college kids, ya know? Kinda cute, ain't he? So anyway, now I gotta sneak him into the shelter tonight, and tomorrow I'll take him downtown, try to get some cash for him."

"Can I hold him, Tim?"

"Awright, just don't let the driver see him. You got any dope?"

"That ain't my scene," said Keith taking the small dog and setting it on his lap.

The pup stretched, looked up at him with deep mournful eyes and what seemed to Keith a hint of a smile.

He stroked the pup's sleek fur and experienced a warm glow in his heart.

Mmmm, see you.

Keith's eyes widened. "What the hell?"

Tim said, "What the hell what?"

Keith looked up from the pup to Tim. "Never mind – nothing."

He looked back down at the pup who was still staring up at him.

Paw stroke nice...like.

Keith raised his hand from the dog.

Not stop...like.

He wondered if some sort of flu bug was getting to him, causing some sort of delirium. He knew it wasn't alcohol or drugs. He never drank in excess anymore, and he had always steered clear of drugs.

"Okay. Give 'im back, Keith," said Tim.

Keith looked up at Tim. "You sure you didn't hear anything?"

"Only thing I heard was you telling me you was broke. Now gimme back my dog."

Reluctantly Keith started to hand the pup back.

Mmmm...nooo. Like you...stay with you!

He hesitated, overwhelmed by the emotion he was picking up. *Yes, that was it,* he thought. *Picking up.* He realized now the voice was inside his mind. It was like a tangle of pictures, and emotions that merged and formed meaning to him. *How could that be?*

"C'mon Keith, give him over."

Tim roughly grabbed the pup from Keith.

Owww! Not like this one.

Tim tucked the dog into his interior coat pocket and

grabbed the garbage bag holding his meager belongings. "My stop, man. I'll be seeing you around."

Keith put a hand on him.

"Hang on, Tim. You want to sell him, don't you? Let me have him right now and tomorrow I'll give you ten bucks I got stashed away. What do you say?"

"Naw, man. I can sell him to one of them college kids tomorrow for twenty or more. You give me ten bucks tonight he's yours, but it's gotta be tonight."

Mmmm...dark. Bad smell...want out.

"Okay Tim, but you got to come out to my camp with me to get it."

Keith figured he had at least twenty dollars buried next to a tree by his makeshift refuge near the Willbury River. He was willing to fork over part of it for the pup.

"Well, if you really got it, okay. If you're bullshitting me I'll put a hurt on you for sure, got it?"

"Yeah, I got it and I'm not shitting you."

Tim sat back down. Both sat until the bus hit its last stop at Craigmore Park.

They got off the bus, shuffled across the dimly lit park into the dense brush and trees that separated it from the river. Tim cursed, stumbling over the thick roots and wet undergrowth that lay under the canopy of tall pine trees.

Keith turned and said, "Why don't you give me the dog, Tim, so if you take a fall he don't get hurt."

Tim replied gruffly, "No way, man. You ain't getting this guy until I get my ten bucks."

They tramped deeper into the underbrush, Keith could *hear* the small pup making complaints. Finally, they arrived at the tiny clearing that held Keith's tarped lean-to and a couple of broken down plastic chairs.

"Have a seat man," said Keith. "I got to go take a piss."

"Okay, cool. I'll wait." Tim plopped into one of the chairs which sagged under his weight.

Keith dipped back into the bushes and crept over to his buried stash. From the muddy ground, he dug out the tin box that held his cash. He stood and started counting bills, so he could bring in just the ten.

Other hurt you! He turned just in time to see Tim's fist coming right at him. He tried to jump back, but he was too late, the punch connected with his face...darkness.

Keith woke sputtering. Rain was pouring on him like a waterfall. He got up unsteadily and staggered back to his camp. The tin box lay open on the ground collecting rain.

Man, what an idiot – damn. Should have told him I would meet him at the shelter with the cash.

Keith briefly thought of going after Tim to get his cash and the dog back, but realized it would be futile. By now the bastard would have spent most of the cash on crappy whiskey or drugs. Tim wouldn't go to the shelter, he would be piss-blind drunk lying in an ally or some dimly lit park downtown. *Shit! Only thing to do is search for him tomorrow.* He crept resignedly under his makeshift lean-to and eventually drifted off, dreaming of little dogs with soulful eyes.

Keith awoke early and crawled out of his shelter. There was a light fog drifting through the forested area around his camp. He cast about for his backpack and found it in some nearby bushes. Tim had given it a going through before throwing it aside, but everything was there still, even the half sandwich he had saved from yesterday.

He sat eating the soggy sandwich and contemplated his plan of action. Keith wanted to get that dog before Tim sold him or abandoned him somewhere. He finished up his meal and started for town.

At the bus stop, he recalled that the absence of cash would require walking to town. It would be about an hour or more before Keith could get to where he imagined he might find Tim. He had no choice – nobody was going to give him a ride. At least the fog had lifted and given way to a warming sunny morning. He picked up his pace to a trot.

It was around ten o'clock when Keith made it downtown to the shelter. He walked in, saw Jim Trelik manning the front check-in counter.

Jim looked up and smiled. "Hey there, Keith. Haven't seen you for quite a spell. You still camping wild out by the Willbury?"

"Hi, Jim. Yeah still got my little camp going. How you doing these days?"

"Aww, can't complain." He squinted at Keith and said, "Man, that is one nasty shiner you got there boss. What happened?"

"I took a tumble last night going out to my place, bad luck for me I guess. Say, is Tim Hudge here by any chance?"

"Tim? Nope he didn't come in last night. Probably got too wasted and bedded down in a dumpster or something. He'll probably show tonight when he gets hungry enough."

Damn!

"Well okay, guess I'll check back this evening. Thanks, Jim."

He gave Jim a wave and headed out, hurrying towards University Avenue.

It was Saturday, and University Avenue with all its trendy shops, bars, and coffee houses was crowded with people. *This is where I'll find him*, he thought.

Keith walked up and down the nine blocks where he figured to find Tim panhandling. He stopped a few times to query street people he knew if they had seen him, but no one had so far today. The sun was now high overhead – sweat began to roll off him. He decided to search some of the alley dumpsters, hoping that Tim perhaps was sleeping off a booze overload courtesy of Keith's stash money. After three tries he found him passed out behind some garbage cans in Knot Alley.

Keith grabbed Tim roughly by the front of his puke stained shirt. "Wake up, asshole! C'mon, wake up!"

Tim's eyes opened blearily. His breath could have knocked out a water buffalo.

"Wha tha fuck?"

Keith slapped him hard. "Where's my money and that dog, shithead."

Tim rubbed at his cheek – his reddened eyes were now wide open.

"Keith, man I hadda get a drink."

Keith threw him back down on the ground.

"I want my dough and the pup, dude, or I'm gonna lay into you real good."

Tim sat up, looking at Keith with fear.

"Man, I spent your cash last night on...you know."

His eyes suddenly lit up. "Wait, Keith, I do got some of your cash." He fumbled in his front pocket and brought out a wrinkled five-dollar bill. With a shaking hand, he offered it up to Keith. "Here man, take it, but don't hurt me. I'm real sorry, man, really."

With a quick sweep of his hand Keith grabbed the bill.

"Where's the dog, Tim? What did you do with him?"

Tim frowned. "These three dudes stole him offa me. I

was trying to sell him to them, but the bastards laughed at me, and slapped me around. One of 'em grabbed the dog and they took off. They all looked like vampires dressed in black or something, I don't know."

Keith looked hard at Tim for a moment and then gave him a quick kick in the face. Tim fell back, out cold.

"That's for last night, and you're damn lucky I don't give you more than that."

He walked away to start another search.

It seemed to Keith he had been all over the town. He had no luck anywhere finding the pup. The futility of his search began to sink in. He sat down on a bench to rest, staring down at his dirty boots in disappointment. It was getting towards evening now – a cool wind began to blow. He was hungry and tired. *Maybe I should just give up. Probably wasn't real anyway.*

Keith gazed up at the evening sky, shrugged, and decided to call it a day. He reached for his pack and noticed an envelope lying against it. *Wind must have blown it*, he thought. He picked it up and peered inside. His eyes widened – it was filled with money.

Keith looked around. There was no one approaching him, nobody searching around in a panic. He got up, headed down a side-street, then turned up a deserted alley. He opened the envelope and pulled out the bills – something else dropped out to the ground. Keith looked down and saw a couple of small, transparent plastic bags containing white powder. He frowned. *Drug money.* Keith counted the bills and discovered he had a hundred dollars, which he pocketed without any remorse. He dropped the envelope, mashed the bags with his boot, and walked away. *Time for a burger.*

Later, Keith stopped at a grocery store and picked up a few large tins of corned beef, a small carton of milk, and a bottle of water. Aboard the bus back to his camp he became edgy and anxious, as if something was scratching at his brain.

Keith got off at his stop, shouldered his pack, and commenced to cross the park. He made it about halfway across the neatly trimmed grass, then abruptly stopped.

Hurrrttt, hurt, hurrrttt...stop hurt me, STOP, HURRTTTS!!

Keith looked wildly about but could see nothing. He decided to try something in desperation. He concentrated and thought, *You where? Show, I find.*

He sensed surprise mixed with terror and pain, then a picture coalesced in his mind.

Keith ran over to the bike path that wove through the park and followed it to the right. He ran at full speed until he reached Riverbend Bridge. There he followed a scrubby little pathway that led him under the bridge. Keith saw three young men standing and laughing around a small fire – they had their backs to him.

"Burn it again," one of them laughed. "Let's make the little fucker really jump."

They were passing a bottle between themselves and by their uneasy stance it looked to Keith they had been at it for a while. One of them picked up a glowing brand and poked at something.

Ahhhhhhhh, no hurt, no, no, NOOO!!

Keith threw down his pack and barreled straight at them. One of the men turned and spotted Keith. Before he could react, Keith knocked him into the other two, sending them sprawling. One landed headfirst in the small fire and began screaming in pain. Keith administered a boot to the back of another's head, who collapsed in a heap. The third looked up at him in terror. Keith hauled him up and threw him into the river. The rapid current carried him downstream with his arms flailing. He looked over at Fire-face who was howling and touching his blistered countenance. The one he had kicked was still out cold. Then he saw the pup.

The dog was tied by a rope around his neck to a rock. He lay on his side breathing heavily, char marks crisscrossed his body. Keith knelt, untied the rope, and gently picked up the pup.

He stood up and turned to Fire-face. "I ever catch any of you around here or anywhere else with a dog you're gonna think what happened to you this time was a stroll in the playground. You understand me, you piece of garbage?"

Fire-face's lips quivered. "Yeyess...I understand."

After retrieving his pack, he trotted off with the pup cradled in his right arm. He wanted to get to camp and take care of the dog's wounds. Keith knew that no veterinarian would come out here for some homeless guy and his injured animal.

The sun was setting when they arrived at his camp. Keith dropped his pack and sat cross legged on the ground with the pup in his lap. The dog weakly lifted its head and looked up at him.

...Friend...nice one...thirsty me...

Keith reached over, opened the backpack and retrieved the bottle of water. He poured some into his cupped hand and held it under the pup's small muzzle. The little guy lapped it up eagerly – Keith poured more until the dog stopped drinking. He tried connecting with the pup as he had done previously.

You hungry?...Food want?

...Mmmm...hunger...yes want eat...

Keith opened a tin of corned beef and fed the dog with his fingers until he stopped accepting any more offerings. He took some water and started to bathe the pup's burns.

Owwww! No, hurt!!

I'm not hurting you to cause pain...I help...clean the hurts... good for you, okay?

Keith could sense the pup understood, but did not like it much. Cleaning the wounds, he noticed with relief that they didn't appear as bad as he had originally thought. He finished ministering to the pup and let him lay down in his lap. Keith ate some of the corned beef and watched the curled-up dog. The pup slept soundly, occasionally whimpering as if having bad dreams. Keith smiled and ran his hand lightly over the dog in reassurance. After a time, Keith carefully lifted the pup into his arm and crawled under the shelter of the tarp. He was putting the dog into his old sleeping bag when he noticed something – the pup was larger than he recalled from the previous night. He thought about it for a moment, shrugged, and crawled in to share the warmth of the bag.

Keith woke to the sound of rain gently drumming on the tarp above his head. The pup was a warm spot by his side. He stretched, and the dog begin to stir.

Mmmmm...warm...good...hungry!

Keith reach down and stroked the pup, then hesitated – something didn't feel right. He unzipped the bag and beheld a much larger dog. He shook his head. It was the same pup, but it had grown almost triple in size. *What the hell!*

Mmmm hell..what are hell?

"Never mind, boy...here I'll get you some food."

Keith opened another can of corned beef and fed the dog. He studied the dog. He recognized the breed from a dog he had seen on a popular television show – a Jack Russell terrier. *Like none in this world, that's for sure*, he thought. Half of the Jack's face was black – including one ear – while the other was pure white. Keith's eyes widened – the dog's burns were gone.

The pup stopped asking for more food and looked up at Keith with eyes that shone with intelligence. Despite the strangeness and a vague sense of alarm, Keith's heart filled with affection.

Mmm...better now...stronger than before. Must see your mind now...let me see.

His eyes, and the thought behind them, compelled Keith. He took a deep breath. A picture of an open door formed in his head. Something shadowy loomed at the doorway, it hesitated briefly then rushed the opening, trying to squeeze through. Keith recoiled in pain and slammed the door.

You hurt me...too much at once...ouch!

The dog looked at him with what appeared to be sympathy. He placed a paw gently on Keith.

Mmmm...I hurt you...not want to...slower again try? Want to learn...must see your mind...must!

Keith felt that compulsion come again, this time he imagined a wall – the urge to open his mind stopped instantly.

We do this on my terms. You not try and order me or I block...okay?

Mmm yes...regret force...want to learn...be slower...better.

Keith looked into the dog's eyes. They did not show malice or deceit, only kindness. He let the door materialize again, ready to slam it shut if needed. He could perceive the shadow, this time it floated in as though carried on a gentle summer breeze. Keith drifted on a white billowy cloud in a vivid blue sky...

Keith blinked...the sun was bright and hot through the tarp. He had been out for hours. He sat up, saw the dog regarding him.

You are awake. This is good. I possessed anxiety that you might not come back from our linking.

Keith could have sworn the pup winked at him. He said, "Your thinking is clearer now, more precise. What happened?"

In your mind I learned. Clearer and better is my speech. I learned all from your mind...partner?

That last word carried an emotion of hope mixed with a need to form a bond. Keith found himself smiling and no longer afraid. He had been out and at the dog's mercy both physically and mentally for hours, but had come to no harm.

Partner, yeah. We are partners. So, what are we going to call you? You need to choose a name, partner.

The pup's eyes twinkled in delight, then a look of concentration. *Name? Oh yes, my title of address. You can see I am still learning...perceiving. Hmmm, name, name, name... what shall I like?*

His eyes went to the tin of corned beef and after a moment brightened.

Hardwicke...that will be my name!

Keith was surprised. He looked from the dog to the can and then picked it up and read the label. *A quality product of Hardwicke Ltd*, is what it said at the bottom. He dropped the can.

"You can read now?"

Of course, I learned from you. Is it not a champion name?

"Uh yeah, but listen here...Hardwicke, if you learned from me, then you know that you aren't like other dogs. That name is a little unusual...how about we shorten it to Hardy? Just when I am talking to you out in public...what do you say?

Hmmm. Yes, your point I take. I must blend in...yes, yes...it will be Hardy when you talk. We must be careful in the public with people. You think at me when you wish to say something... okay? Not talk other than to call my name and other things people say to dogs.

"Good idea...whoops." *Good idea...Hardwicke.*

Keith grinned. His communication with Hardy was getting smoother and taking much less effort. It was as if he was developing a mental muscle that grew stronger as he exercised it. He also felt a bonding – a growing closer to the dog – like finding a lost soulmate.

So, Hardwicke, how is it that you can do this mind thing... and the healing as well? Are you from this planet?

Keith could sense amusement from Hardy, and worry.

I cannot say how I came about...it is puzzling to me as well, but I think I was...manipulated? Is that the word? I am of this world...created? No, I was born of parents...yes...parents, mother and father.

There was a sadness in his thoughts.

Yes, yes, I remember mother, father. Taken away from them

by people, me and my siblings were. They used a needle on each of us to kill, then all of us were put in a box and thrown away like refuse! My siblings were murdered by these people. They thought I was dead too, but I was stronger, more powerful... healed myself, like with the burns.

The last thought held a rage that burned in Keith's head. He thought he knew the answer to Hardwicke's origin now, though.

Tim found you after a man from Barrett Laboratories chucked the box into a dumpster. You came from those labs... an experiment that went wrong? I'm glad you came out of it alright, Hardy.

Keith felt the rage turn into warmth. It looked as though Hardy was smiling at him.

I too am glad and I am joyful we found each other. Other minds I can see into, but not...talk. We have a connection... partner...it is good!

Now it seemed the grin was turning into a frown of concentration. Keith was about to ask what was troubling him when...

We need to leave this place very soon. Barrett people might find out about me. We need...money? Yes, money so we can go. Money for purchase of transportation to get away. How can this be achieved? Wait...

Hardy's eyes brightened, the grin came back.

Crowley's...card game... gamble...yes, yes! You have money now, Keith/partner?

I got maybe sixty bucks, yeah, but Hardy...gambling I stopped...made me lose everything. Don't want to go back to nothing.

Hardy placed a paw on Keith's arm and stared into his eyes.

You take me with you...this time you win! Trust your partner?

Keith thought about it for a moment. What did he have to lose anyway? He nodded to the dog.

Okay, what the hell. Let me eat something though, I am starving. Then we'll have to walk in to town...you're too big to hide now.

I agree partner. Hungry I am again too, but first I fix the hurt on your face. He watched the dog raise its paw and then felt an electric-like shock as it contacted his bruised face.

There now...it is away...no more hurting?

Keith grabbed his small shaving mirror and saw there was no mark – the pain was gone. He was dumbfounded.

Hardy pawed him. *Let us eat, partner and journey to town.*

Keith walked into Crowley's with Hardy on a makeshift leash of rope. He saw Patty the barmaid and sketched a small salute towards her.

"Hey, Patty, how are things?"

She looked him up and down with a smile.

"Not too bad for an old gal. Where you been hiding, Keith? Ain't seen you 'round for quite a spell."

"Aww, you know, just trying to stay out of trouble. Say, is it okay to bring my dog?"

She looked down at Hardwicke, who grinned up at her with his tail wagging. A true image of a flirt.

"Ohhhh, now ain't he just the sweetest thing you ever did see?" She came around from the bar and knelt to give Hardy pets and some scratches behind the ears. Keith could feel Hardy enjoying the attention, especially the scratches.

"What's his name, Keith? I think we can just say that he is a service dog and leave it at that...what a cutie!!"

"His name is Hardy. Thanks, Patty."

"No problemo, Keith." She frowned and said, "You thinking about the cards again, aren't you? You know you ain't got the luck, Keith. How 'bout a beer instead? I even got some treats for your little buddy."

"Uh, well thanks, Patty, but I got a good feeling this time that my luck has changed. I'll take you up on the beer, though, and I'm sure Hardy might like a little something."

She shook her head and said, "You always say that, Keith, and then you end up without a dime. Well, this one beer is on the house 'cause you'll be broke in an hour."

Patty went back behind the bar and drew Keith a brew. She put it on the bar along with a biscuit for Hardy. Keith bent down and gave the treat to Hardy who sniffed it.

This is not the corned beef! What food is this?

Keith kept the biscuit in front of the dog and thought: *This is what dogs like. Go ahead and eat it for appearances sake, anyway.*

Reluctantly Hardy ate the treat.

Keith was still worried about the plan.

Hardy, I hope you are right about this.

There was no reply from Hardy. Keith could feel him concentrating very hard.

He thanked Patty again and made for the poker room in the back. He opened the door and led Hardy through. Keith surveyed the room. There were only two tables working, one was full, the other had open seats. He walked over to the table with a vacancy. He recognized one of the players, a man dressed in a black leather vest, a flowery cowboy shirt, and black Stetson. Delbert Bronkowski had separated Keith from his cash many times before. Bronkowski looked up at him and gave him a wide smile.

"There's my favorite sucker! How you doing, Keith my man?"

"I'm doing okay, Del. Can I sit in?"

"You got money, you can play. Is what I always say." Delbert looked down at the dog.

"Hey, that's a nice-looking pup. What's its name?"

"His name is Hardy," Keith said as he sat down. "Usual rules?"

Delbert nodded. "Yep, five buck ante, five buck limit raises on each go around. Ya want bigger play, the other table has higher stakes."

"This will suit me okay," said Keith. "Let's play some cards." He threw in his five dollars and placed the rest of his poke on the table in front of him.

Delbert smiled. "This here is Keith, boys. Keith, meet Charley, Bob, and Herb."

Everyone nodded at Keith. Charley held the deck and called out that it would be five card draw, no wild, and proceeded to deal.

Keith waited until all five of his cards had been dealt, then picked them up. He had a pair of jacks, and that was it.

"Dealer opens for two bucks," said Charley, frowning over his cards.

Delbert was next. "I'll be raising that by three bucks."

Everyone tossed in their money. Charley asked who wanted cards.

Keith asked for three when it was his turn. He did not get any improvement to his hand.

Images came into his head...

Look partner, look, I see through their eyes.

Keith was electrified. What he saw was like a hazy live multiscreen video. He could view each man's hand!

"Dealer opens for three bucks," said the still frowning Charley.

Delbert said, "Cost all of ya five total to stay in this man's game."

Keith stifled a grin – Delbert had a pair of threes and the others were holding garbage.

Everybody started to fold, and Delbert's smile got bigger until...

"Call you, Delbert," said Keith as he put in his five. "What do you got?"

Delbert laid them down with a slight frown. That expression got more pronounced as the evening wore on.

Four hours later and seven-hundred dollars richer, Keith and Hardy departed Crowley's. It had been a very profitable night indeed. Delbert and the others were not exactly happy, but they took it in stride. "Luck of the draw. I'll get ya next time out," Delbert said with a laugh.

It was around 10 p.m. now and Keith was pretty hungry.

I too would like food, partner.

Keith grinned and reached down to give Hardy a scratch behind the ear.

Understood, partner. Say, we are flush, so how about I get us a room at Motel 9 out by the highway? They allow dogs and there are some fast food joints right next door.

I agree with this plan, my friend. To acquire good shelter and warm food is most welcome.

As they made their way to the motel, Keith reflected on his conversations with Hardwicke. He was pleasantly surprised to find that they had spoken as equals, not as master and dog. He accepted the idea – it was totally natural and right.

After they had gotten a room Keith told Hardwicke to make himself comfortable while he went to get food for them. Jokingly Keith asked what he wanted.

I wish to have the french-fries and a double cheeseburger... hold the pickles and onions. From what your mind tells me, they look delicious!

Keith could feel a playful mirth with those thoughts. He shook his head and smiled at Hardy. "You got it, my man!"

Later, stuffed and content, they relaxed on the soft bed. Hardy burped.

Most satisfying, say I. We must partake of the onion rings and the barbeque chicken sandwich with Swiss cheese on the next foray. He burped again.

Keith burst out in laughter. "I think maybe some bacon and eggs would be more appropriate in the morning."

Hmmm...Yes, that sounds very delectable indeed. Perhaps with the hash brown potatoes as well?

"Perfect," said Keith.

Hardy got up, stretched, and looked at Keith.

Tomorrow we return to Crowley's and continue to gain more dollars. I suggest we play the...bigger stakes table? More money we must have to journey far away from this place.

"Okay partner. I'm all in. It'll take us a few days, then we should have enough to buy a car and have enough money for traveling as well. I don't know about you, but I have always dreamt of the Oregon coast. Not so many people and it is far away from where we are now. I also hear there are casinos there too."

By one of the great oceans – far from large cities and prying eyes, plus a revenue stream. This sounds ideal.

Hardwicke stretched again and jumped down from the bed.

I must go for some relief before sleep. Up with you, lackadaisical partner!

The next morning Keith woke up and found Hardy on the pillow next to him. He blinked in amazement. Hardwicke had grown bigger again. The dog opened his eyes and looked at Keith.

I feel quite strong now. Soon I will run in ocean water!

After breakfast and a welcome hot shower, Keith went down and paid the motel clerk for another night. It was wonderful to have a roof overhead and actual plumbing again. He whistled as he went back up to their room. Life was taking a fantastic turn – he felt great.

Keith opened the door and looked for Hardy.

Where are you Hardwicke? No reply.

He went to the bathroom for a look...not there. Starting to worry, he looked under the bed and even in the cheap wardrobe. No Hardy.

Hardy! Hardy, where are you? Hardy!

There was a click at the front door lock. He turned and watched as the door slowly opened. In pushed Hardwicke with a big grin on his muzzle.

Greetings partner! Relieved and refreshed am I, and so for the day's proceedings am prepared.

Keith was mystified. "How in the heck did you get out, or for that matter, back in?"

He could sense amusement coming from Hardwicke.

Simple, after I figured it out in my head. I am stronger...New things I can do...manipulate things. The door and its mechanism, an easy thing.

Keith closed the door and looked back at Hardy.

New things I can do...heh!

Keith plopped down on the bed and Hardwicke jumped up next to him. Absently he ran his hand over the dog's head and back.

Ahh, a little behind the ear please...no the other one. Mmmm just so, yes.

Hardy put a paw on Keith.

To Crowley's we go, but not until later. First for you, partner, new clothes and foot protection..errr...shoes I mean. You will feel...more confident? People will not look at you so...downward?

Keith laughed. "You trying to tell me something partner? Well you're right, I am a bit on the crusty side. Okay, but we need to stop in at the *Furry Friend's* shop, so we can get you looking respectable as well."

Hours later back in the motel room Keith changed into a new set of clothes and comfortable boots. He had also stopped for a haircut and shave at Ron's Barbershop, where everyone had commented on how fine a dog Hardy was. Hardy sported a nice black leather collar and leash Keith had purchased from *Furry Friend's*, he had also bought some dry dog food. Keith put some in his hand for Hardy who sniffed it and turned up his nose.

This is not the Swiss cheese barbeque chicken sandwich... nor the onion rings either. Swill this is...you eat it.

Keith shrugged and put the kibble in a trashcan. It dawned on him again that he was not dealing with a typical dog. Hardwicke was like another race altogether that just happened to look like a dog.

"Okay partner, I get it, but when we get to Oregon and get settled we're gonna get off the junk food and eat better. Steak, chicken, or pork chops sound good?"

Agreed, but the T-bone steak for me. Now come, laggard, off with us to Crowley's!

They walked into Crowley's. Patty looked over and brightened when she saw them.

"Well, well, aren't we looking good this evening? Damn, Keith, if I was ten years younger I'd make a play for you."

He grinned in an aww shucks kind of way. "You're gonna make me blush, Patty. Anyway, I thought you were ten years younger than me."

"Oh, go on with you, you sweet talker. Heard you did pretty good last night. You coming back for more?"

"Yep, sure am. I'm feeling pretty lucky right now. How about a beer?"

"Coming up!" She paused and looked at Hardwicke again. "Darn, he looks bigger than yesterday. That is Hardy, right?"

"Yep, same Hardy all right. Maybe he looks bigger 'cause he just ate."

Patty shook her head and shrugged. "Maybe, maybe so. Do you think he wants a treat?"

No dry cardboard for me!

"Uh, no he's fine, Patty. Thanks anyway."

Keith took his beer and they made their way to the poker room. He saw there was space at the higher stakes table. The owner, Harry Crowley, was sitting in as the house dealer. He was grossly overweight and the tight button-down shirt he wore magnified it even more. Keith walked over and waited for Crowley to look up and acknowledge him.

He gave Keith a pretty condescending smile. "Evening, Keith. You maybe picked the wrong table? Lower play is over where Delbert and the rest are at." Keith smiled back at him.

"Nope, this is the table for me tonight. I'm feeling really lucky these days."

Crowley looked him up and down. "Well you sure look cleaned up. It takes two hundred to buy in and you can keep buying chips if you get low. You got that much?"

"Yep," Keith said, sitting down. He pulled his cash from his pocket and counted out the two hundred. Crowley smiled, gave him chips, and introduced him around the table.

"Five stud, no wild," Crowley said as he began to deal.

You got them, partner?

No doubt there is. I have them...look.

Keith smiled – the evening began.

Hours later there were only three people remaining at the table. Keith had amassed a large pile of chips. Crowley wasn't looking so happy, neither was the other player. Crowley looked up at the clock.

"Got time for one more game before we have to close. You two game for a no limit round?"

The other player, Toby Willmont, thought about it for a moment, checked his wallet, and then nodded in the affirmative. Keith smiled and said, "Sure thing, I'm game."

"Okay then, let's make it five card draw, no wild, no limit." Crowley had a faint smile as he dealt the cards.

Keith picked up his cards. He had two kings, an ace, and a pair of twos. He got the relay from Hardwicke and saw that Willmont had a pair of fours and nothing else. Crowley had a pair of aces, a nine, and a pair of threes.

"Your open, Toby," said Crowley.

"Open for one hundred."

Keith could barely restrain a laugh. He threw in the same – Crowley raised the ante.

"Gonna cost ya five hundred more to draw cards, gentlemen."

Toby scowled, but threw in. Keith did the same.

Crowley looked at Toby. "How many you want?"

Toby took three cards and got a four of clubs. Now he had three of a kind.

Keith took one card, getting rid of the ace. He got another king. Full house!

Crowley stood pat.

"To you, Toby," he said.

Toby threw in two hundred. Keith raised two hundred.

Crowley looked at Keith for a moment, then smiled.

"See that and raise you one thousand."

Toby threw in his cards. "I fold, goddamn it!"

Keith said, "See that and raise you another thousand."

Crowley smiled and tossed in more chips. "I think I'm gonna call you, Keith. Whatta ya got?"

Keith turned his cards. "Full house, kings over twos."

Partner...Keith! The Crowley has done something, changed a card.

Through Hardy's eyes Keith saw that another ace had replaced the nine in Crowley's hand. He had cheated! What could he do now? He sure couldn't flat out accuse Crowley of cheating, nobody here would buy that.

He sensed intense energy emanating from Hardy – it washed over him in waves. Crowley smiled broadly, and laid out his cards. "Must not be your night after all, Keith. Read 'em and weep!"

He resigned himself to being had and looked at the cards. Then he started to laugh.

"Well gee, Harry, you sure are a comedian when you want to be."

Crowley looked puzzled.

"What are you talking about, Keith? I got you beat. Aces over threes takes your hand any day."

Toby burst out laughing. "Yeah, Harry, it sure would if ya had it!"

Crowley stopped smiling and looked down at his hand. His eyes widened in disbelief. He was holding two aces, a pair of threes, and a nine.

"Looks like you took that nine for an ace, Harry," Toby cackled.

Harry Crowley looked as though steam would vent out his ears as he watched Keith rake in the chips.

"Looks like it was my night after all," Keith said grinning.

He felt quite a bit of merriment from Hardy lying under the table.

Crowley very reluctantly cashed him out to the tune of six thousand dollars. When Keith stood up to leave, Crowley got up and blocked his way.

"I don't think I want to be seeing you back here again, Keith. You take my meaning? You and that mutt are bad for business."

Keith stared hard at Harry Crowley. "No worries, Harry old pal. I was getting tired of this crappy poker room anyway. Now get out of my way. You take *my* meaning, fat man?"

Crowley blinked and backed off. Keith gave a very surprised Patty a one hundred dollar tip on the way out.

Back at the motel room Hardwicke and Keith enjoyed a late meal.

The onion rings... so crispy they are. The barbeque chicken with Swiss cheese...sublime!

Keith laughed. "Next time we'll go for T-bones partner. Say, tell me again how you managed that trick on Crowley."

Not a trick...the nine was in his shirt. I...made it move back... not move...shifted in space...yes! The ace I made go away to nothing...hard...hurt my head.

"Well I'm gonna always remember the look on his face when he saw what he had turned over."

Yes, I thought his brain would...detonate? It was quite gratifying to...get his goat?

"Yeah, that's it." Keith laughed hard, and in his mind he felt the same emotion from Hardwicke. He looked at Hardy and thought to himself how good it felt being with him. They were not simply partners – it was much more than that – they were friends.

Friends, yes...we two are bonded and it is good.

Keith gave him a scratch behind the ear. "Yes, my friend, it is very good."

The next morning Keith looked at Hardy who was stretching at the end of the bed.

"Say, my man. You haven't gotten any bigger."

I am where I will remain now...no more do I grow in body.

"Well I hope you still got a full lifespan ahead...I mean you aged pretty fast up to this point." Keith could feel a hesitation coming from the dog. He looked in Hardy's eyes, it looked as though they were filled with a sadness. Abruptly the emotions closed off.

It will be well, my friend, do not...sweat it?

Keith looked at him a moment longer. "Yeah that's the word. I am glad all is well."

As I am...Shall we begin our quest?

The two set out to the east side of town. At Brad Pinkler's used car lot Keith found a reliable looking small van for two thousand dollars. He was glad he still had a valid driver's license as the two of them drove away. He glanced over at Hardwicke who was sitting happily in the front passenger seat.

"Well, buddy, we got wheels and now we can make tracks. Do you still like the idea of Oregon?"

Indeed, yes...the ocean air...lots of space. Yes, let us proceed and be merry.

Keith laughed. "Merrily we roll along! First thing, though, is get this van registered and some plates so we are all legal. We also got to get some supplies for the road."

Hardwicke was not happy about having to wait in the car while Keith was in the DMV getting things straight. After taking care of the vehicle Keith stopped at a Minit-Mart to get supplies. Hardy sent him a suggestion: *Something with a bone in it please. I still have the urge to chew things.*

Your wish is my command Hardwicke, old pal. Keith shot back.

Keith bought water, assorted snacks, and a T-bone for Hardy. He also purchased an ice chest and a bag of ice to keep things cool. After he loaded everything into the van, he said, "Well how about we stop off at Craigmore Park? We can have some food and I can grab a couple of things I left out at my old camp."

That is acceptable, partner. Then to the road and Oregon.

"Yep, that's the plan, my friend."

Keith pulled into the parking area of Craigmore Park. He thought how abruptly things had changed, how happy he had become. It was not the money – though that helped – it was having a real friend after all these years. He was no longer alone in the world. That was the true source of his happiness now.

Hardy and Keith went over to a bench and made a meal of some chips and beef sticks, washed down with some bottled water.

These beef sticks...interesting, chewy, but not like real meat, not like cheeseburgers.

"Yeah, you'll like that T-bone a hell of a lot more when we stop driving tonight."

After lunch, they walked into the brush towards Keith's old camp. Keith thought it was amazing what can happen in a couple of days. They came to the clearing. To Keith it seemed ages since he had been here. He was glad it would be the last time.

"Just have to dig up another little box. It's got some old pictures of me and my parents."

Parents, yes. Where are your parents Keith?

"Oh, they passed away years ago. Drunk driver ran a light and...well they were in the wrong place. What about yours?"

Mine...they are...at the lab still...I hear them at times, like a faint whisper in my mind. They warn never to come near...I would be taken and destroyed.

Keith put a hand on Hardy's head and gave him a stroke.

"Is there something we can do? I expect that lab is pretty secure, but maybe..."

No, they are correct. I believe they too will soon be ended by those lab men...cruel, cold, men. Not like you, my friend. No, we go to Oregon and be free, we must be free.

Keith retrieved the box and they made their way back

through the undergrowth to the park. They walked by the few cars in the parking lot to the van. Keith fished in his pocket for the keys.

Beware!! Trouble comes.

He whirled – it was the three who had hurt Hardy. Fire-face had a gun. Hardwicke leaped into the air in front of Keith.

Two shots rang out. Keith dove sideways, rolled, and charged the group, but they were already running to an old sedan. They jumped in and peeled out. Keith forgot about them, he turned back to his friend. Hardy was lying in a pool of blood. He ran to the dog's side and knelt.

"Hardy! Come on, man, stay with me." *Hardwicke, partner, friend, don't go, don't leave!*

There was nothing – Hardy was not breathing.

Tears streaming down his face, he gently picked up the dog. Keith had to go – someone had surely called the cops – but he wasn't going to leave his friend here in a parking lot. He placed Hardy in the back seat, got in the van and drove away. When Keith reached the State highway, he turned west – towards Oregon.

He drove for hours in a state of shock and loss. The world was like a black void. Keith had found joy and friendship with Hardwicke, now with two gunshots it was all gone. On he drove, his mind a blank. Finally, he stopped for gas. He looked in the window at the small body lying on the back seat as he pumped the fuel. He choked back tears. When he had filled the tank, he took a shirt from his old backpack and covered Hardy. Keith decided he would bury his friend in Oregon, somewhere near the coast. He returned to the highway and headed west, into the moonless black night.

• • •

Keith sat in an old wicker rocker and regarded the rugged Oregon coast from the covered porch of his home. The house was of timber construction and perched on six forested acres that gave way to stunning views of the ocean. He passed a hand through silvery hair...how long had he been in Oregon now? He figured it was fifty years... *Fifty years? How could the time have passed by so fast?* He felt his heart hesitate a beat or two – time was short, he knew it. He didn't want to go yet, there was too much happening in the world.

The whole globe was on the brink of an all-out nuclear war – any day or hour the end could come. Russia and most of Europe had already been reduced to radioactive slag, most of the remaining countries had their fingers on the launchers. It passed his mind that if he went now it might be better after all, but no, there were other considerations. He still had work to do.

Keith's thoughts drifted back to the time when he was homeless, existing at the bottom of the barrel. Hardy had come along and changed everything. The dog had saved Keith and set him on the right path once and for all. Then, the shooting. It was all so sharp in his mind, as if it had all happened just last week.

He had driven on like a madman until he reached Oregon. Just before coming out of the coastal mountains, he turned off on a dirt road. Keith followed the rocky track surrounded by dense forest until it ended. He got out and grabbed the small shovel he had purchased the previous day. Trembling, he picked up the wrapped body of his friend and began hiking up an old deer track. Eventually the woods gave way to a clearing that overlooked the ocean – he nodded and commenced digging.

The sun was low over the ocean by the time he finished excavating the grave. He picked up Hardy and lovingly laid him down in the earth. For a long while Keith looked down at his friend, then he sighed and began to cover him over with the moist earth...

Good thing I stopped you right then. Came an amused thought that brought Keith back to the present. He smiled. "You're damn right about that, my friend. I was sure you were dead and gone."

It did take me quite a bit to come back, but I must say I had perfect timing. It would have been very inconvenient to dig myself out of that hole, then search all over for your unappealing human face.

"Well, it would have taken you quite a while. You could only send me a weak thought at the time. If I remember correctly it took about another two weeks for you to really come back full on."

Yes, it took a while, but I recovered.

Keith smiled. "Yep, then you picked those swell numbers for the MegaBoom lottery."

That took a lot out of me to manipulate those numbers from so far away, quite tiring. The look on your face, partner, was quite comical when you found we had won one hundred and fifty million dollars. Yes, it has gone very well for us indeed, old man. Now we have a pack of twenty, there will be more generations to come.

Two years ago, Hardwicke made it known he desired a mate. Keith had taken him on numerous visits to various breeders, finally he had selected a very intelligent female

Jack Russell. She had not possessed the capacities that Hardy had, but the pups came out with his abilities – almost.

...I will be there for the generations to come.

Keith regarded his friend. He had not aged a day in all this time. Keith now knew why Hardwicke had looked so sad long ago when he told Keith all would be well and not to sweat it. He had known even then of his immortality – knew the day would come when his friend would be taken by old age. Hardy could heal wounds and minor things for Keith, but he could not save him from the march of time. Keith would die while Hardwicke continued through the ages.

It is so. The others of the pack do not have immortality. It will be to me to advise, to guide. This war will destroy much of the world. I will lead the pack and perhaps they will find their human counterparts as I found in you. If any of your kind survives, that is.

Keith felt deeply for his partner. Hardy would watch as his children, their children, and so on passed away into faded memory. He would be alone.

You know that it need not be this way...there is...the Choice.

Keith's heart did a double skip before resuming a semi-normal beat. What Hardy said scared him. He did not want to think about it.

Be at peace my friend, do not worry so. Let us watch the sunset over the ocean together as we have done for so many years now.

Hardwicke jumped up into Keith's lap and offered up an ear for scratching.

A little bit to the right...ahhh, that's it. Yes...

Keith dozed off as the red sun sank into the ocean. Hardy remained with him as if keeping a vigil. The voices of the pack whispered in his head wanting to know if the time had come. He kindly dismissed them all. He knew they were all concerned for Keith – telling them the time would come when it would come.

The next morning Keith woke feeling quite well. He got up, went into the kitchen and found the pack had already taken their breakfasts of T-bone steaks from the refrigerator. Although most now hunted for wild meat, they all liked the steaks Keith kept for them.

It is too bad they have not experienced the sublime barbeque chicken sandwich with Swiss cheese, and the french-fries.

Keith smiled and said, "Maybe we ought to rectify that today. How about you and I drive down to the beach later, have a nice walk, and then pick up a bunch of fast food for them? Hell, you never know when that damned war will end all of that. Whatta ya say, partner?"

It sounds typical of your crazy mind, but as you say, who knows what will happen next. Let us go in the afternoon. A stop at the beach will be quite fine indeed.

There were few people about on the long strip of sand that ran on for miles. The sun sparkled on the waves as they crashed against the shore. The two friends walked along undisturbed as the frothing surf made tentative plays for feet and paws. They came upon a big log that had been pitched up on shore, Keith took a seat on it.

"I'm a little winded, Hardy." He stared out over the waves. "Damn, seems like only the other day you and me were flat out running down this beach. The time, it just slipped right by, didn't it?"

But it was GOOD time, my friend. Many memories, much joy together. I regret not one hour of it.

Keith got up and said, "Well, I expect we still have some time left. How about we head back and go get some junk food for the pack?"

Suddenly everything blurred. Keith's heart hammered rapidly in his chest, as if it wanted to pound right through his ribs. He fell back and slid to a sitting position against the log. He could just make out Hardwicke staring intently into his eyes.

It is time, my friend. You must now choose before it is too late.

Keith gasped, "I'm scared. What if it doesn't work?"

Then we both will have lost, but not for want of trying. Please, my friend, trust me as you have always done.

Keith felt his heart stop. He was slipping away – there was nothing to lose. *You're right. Do it!*

Hardy raised a paw to Keith's forehead – he felt a slight shock...blackness.

● ● ●

Two hours later Sheriff Lars Parkington and his deputy stood over a body slumped against a log.

"It's that feller with all the dogs. Looks like his ticker done blown out," said Parkington. The deputy nodded and said, "Well he picked the perfect time for it, now that all hell is breaking loose."

They turned in the direction of town as sirens began to wail. Normally the alarm was meant for tsunamis – this time it was for death coming from the sky.

"That is one correct statement, young man. Better to go like that than what is coming. Hopefully we can ride it out okay, or at least somebody on this damned planet can." He shuffled his foot in the sand. "Okay, we gotta carry him back to the car, the paramedics already got their hands full trying to set up in the emergency shelter. Best we can do right now is take him back to town quickly and store him in the cold room at the Tap House. If we come out of this mess okay, we'll bury him later." They picked up the body and struggled through the sand towards their patrol car. Neither noticed the dog watching them from nearby rocks.

The car sped away, lights flashing madly. The dog trotted out from hiding and stood regarding the pounding surf.

It is well they have taken the husk away.

Keith watched the ocean's ebb and flow through new eyes.

Yes, partner, it was strange seeing my body. I am glad they removed it so scavengers could not savage it – not that it matters now. We are as one – together – truly partners. How could I ever have been afraid of this...union? Hardwicke/Keith looked up at the multitude of streaks crossing the sky. *A new world will be born of fire. We must return to the pack – there is much to prepare for.*

The last beams of the setting sun illuminated a small dog trotting along the beach and into a new beginning.

HEART'S WISH

Toby strode jauntily along the silent forest's path wearing his finest silver clothes. The sun above him shone like a bright gold coin in the blue cloudless sky. *A fine day to escort me fair Sianna to the Saint Quibbler's Day festival in the village*, he thought. He patted the jacket pocket that held a gold ring. *Today will be the day I ask her to be mine. She will come home with me and dwell no more near that dreadful pond in the forest.* He began to whistle merrily as he traversed the winding path.

Toby rounded a corner and stopped whistling. Before him stood a three-meter high black squirrel sitting back on its haunches. It bowed at him.

"Greetings, young master. I am Nozzle, as magical a giant squirrel as can ever be. I have been awaiting you."

Toby was taken aback, but only for a moment.

"And greetings to you as well, Nozzle. I am Toby. Why, pray tell, would ye be waiting for me?"

Nozzle twitched his tail and danced a squirrelly jig.

"Ah, indeed. It is your lucky day today. I have been bound by the forest elementals to come and grant you your heart's wish. Say what it may be, and I shall grant it."

Toby stroked his chin and shuffled a silver boot in the dirt. He had heard vague stories concerning these large rodents. *Something about being tricky*, he thought.

"I am honored, Nozzle, but why would forest elementals want to grant me anything?"

The squirrel replied, "Oh, these matters are above my humble pay grade, master Toby. Perhaps they are grateful for your whistling and the jolly sunlight that reflects off your attire. Who can say? They have promised to make me a fine dinner for performing this task, so happily will I comply."

He pointed at a large stump by the roadside and winked.

"What say you, Toby? Step onto yon woody stage and make known your wish."

Toby thought very hard. *I must be very direct in my wish and leave no leeway for trickery.*

After a moment he smiled and leaped onto the stump.

"My heart's wish is to be desired and enjoyed by my fair Sianna until the end of my days."

Nozzle twitched his tufted ears and waved his paws.

"So it shall be, until the end of your days."

● ● ●

Hours later Sianna came wandering along the forest path.

She muttered to herself, "Where can that Toby be? He should have met me on the path hours ago."

Sianna paused by a nearby stump and was delighted to discover a gold ring lying next to a silver-wrapped chocolate bar. She laughed and looked around expectantly.

"Come out trickster, you know how much I love chocolate."

The forest remained silent. Sianna shrugged and said, "Suit yourself then, I'll just enjoy this chocolate and wait."

She was licking the last of the confection off her fingers when Nozzle appeared.

"Perfect. I have fulfilled my task. Toby has been desired and enjoyed by you until his days ended. A pity it was only a day, but a wish is a wish."

He laughed merrily at Sianna, revealing nasty sharp teeth.

"And now time for my reward. I love a good exotic dinner, especially stuffed with chocolate."

Sianna calmly put on the gold ring and began to shimmer.

Nozzle gulped and watched as she changed into a huge two-headed, warty toad. It gave him two wicked smiles and began to croak at him.

"Yes, as we promised, we will make you a fine dinner."

Both its heads looked at one another.

"Roasted squirrel with a dash of pepper and garlic; an excellent complement to the chocolate appetizer. Yes, he will make a fine dinner indeed."

MR. TIDLEY AND THE BONEMAN: IN PURSUIT OF THE BLACK CHICKEN

"Hey partner wake up. C'mon, Tidley, we've made orbit on Meddy Rex."

Reluctantly I opened my eyes and regarded the Boneman, who was dancing all about my sleeping couch in the most irritating way. Without a word I hopped down and made my way to *The Wilted Lily's* control cabin. My ears pricked up and my nose twitched while I regarded the forward view screen. Medivus Rex looked to be a typical T-5 re-form for carbon-based life. This one had a rose-colored moon. The planet looked gray and gloomy – I didn't like it already.

Boneman said, "I'll get them on the com and get the okay to grav in. Ohhh, we're gonna get that Black Chicken and be rich, Tidley. I can dang well see those CelCreds pouring in now."

I turned and looked at him with a frown. He danced around with glee.

"That's *Mr.* Tidley, Bonehead. Please control yourself and stop that pirouetting."

"It's Boneman gosh darn it, and I'm sorry, *Mr.* Tidley.

Say, don't you have a first name or something? I mean most folks do after all."

The com buzzed. There was no image on the screen, but a voice said, "This be Medivus Rex, who comes hither?"

I waved my paw over the console.

"This is the vessel *Wilting Lily* requesting permission to grav in."

There was a brief pause, then, "Follow you the beam to Port Hrothgar spaceport, do not from the path deviate, mind, or tragedy shall befall you and your interplanetary conveyance. Come apace now, hasten."

Other than Port Hrothgar, the entire planet was cloaked in a damper field and computer grid that stopped any technology from working. If we deviated from that beam, the Lily would plummet down to the planet like a flaming lead brick. Boneman set the ship on auto so it would grab the beam and follow it in.

Medivus Rex was a throwback orbit meant to resemble life in a human Middle-Ages theme, knights, swords, castles, rotting meat, blood – you get the picture. I read that there was also a way – for those with the talent – to manipulate the planet's core computer system to make what would seem to be magic. Personally, I think that whoever designed worlds like this one had a tendency to embellish quite a bit on the actual records that survived from old earth.

"Gonna be darn hard speaking their lingo," said Boneman.

He sat back with his forehead furrowed in concentration, then got up and went to a locker.

"Better see if I got a weapon that'll work on that dang planet."

Soon I could hear swearing and things banging around. I returned my attention to the view screen. Med Rex loomed larger and I thought about how at times the universe can deliver all sorts of flitzing conundrums.

● ● ●

On Guillaume 9 I had owned a profitable bar and gaming house called the Stinking Pilgrim in the bustling frontier town of Blaxstadde ve Tardre. Sure, I had been getting a little bored, but life was, on the whole, quite comfortable. Of course, there were a few run-ins with some characters who habituated my establishment – totally unavoidable in my business.

My hasty departure from Guillaume 9 was due to a misunderstanding with a particularly nasty Umvornian, who had the notion that he would chop off one of my paws. That's when the Boneman – an aspiring bounty hunter – stumbled in, saving my appendage, and probably my life.

The Umvornian, his associates, and, unfortunately, a Centurionem Peace Keeper from the Central Unity of Peace and Intergalactic Egalitarian Sanguinity (CUPIES), had come to untimely ends during the dispute. Life would soon begin to get rather uncomfortable for me, so I accepted Boneman's offer of a lift off Guillaume 9. Reluctantly – for my part – we formed a business relationship in which we would pursue a criminal with the unlikely name of the Black Chicken who was residing on Medivus Rex. Our aim was to collect the sizable reward the barons, earls, and dukes of Medivus Rex placed on the villain's head. There was also a quite substantial reward for him that CUPIES was offering.

• • •

The Boneman returned with a large hammer.

"Looks like this is the only non-tech thing I got, other than my boot dagger, that is. What do you got?"

I looked up at him.

"Keep the dagger and put the tool back. We will acquire the correct weaponry and accompanying accoutrement at Port Hrothgar."

We eventually set down in the domed port of Port Hrothgar. Before locking down *The Wilting Lily* I grabbed a razor sharp Quonietzi slash dagger from my pack and tucked it in my belt – no reason for me to be totally dependent on the local weaponry, after all. Before we disembarked, I admonished my bone-noggin associate to mind his tongue with the port officials.

The enclosed dome was a relic – over a century old at best – it looked to be held together with old Vrock hide. I noticed several other crafts parked near ours and hoped none had come on the same business as we had. We made our way across the tarmac to a door which had a title above emblazoned in gilded letters proclaiming: *Geld*. Being as how it was the only door with a title, we entered.

It was a narrow high-ceilinged room, dimly illuminated by torches in heavy iron sconces every five paces or so along both walls. At the far end, sitting behind a large wooden desk, was an ancient human wearing heavy robes with a red cowl covering his hair. He was busily scribbling something on a roll of paper with a long quill pen. Behind him was a massive oak door with scrolled iron hinges. We approached the official and waited to be acknowledged.

Finally, he paused and from beneath bushy white

eyebrows regarded us with a faint scowl. "I am Craithlbert, the collector of geld-tax and gatekeeper for Port Hrothgar. What be your business at Medivus Rex? Are ye traders of goods from the worlds of CUPIES or beyond? If so, present your goods for inspection and pay the geld." He paused, and his face darkened. "Or be ye scoundrels come from the wild orbits up to some manner of knavery?"

Boneman cleared his throat to answer. Before he could, I turned and hissed at him, "Be silent, oafish Bonebrain. I will address his excellency."

I turned back toward the official and gave him my most sweeping bow.

"Greetings your worship. I am titled Mr. Tidley of House Jacks Russell, and this human is The Boneman. We have come to capture the villain known to you as the Black Chicken."

Craithlbert started to laugh.

"And what be your qualifications, Tidley? Ye look to be of too diminutive a nature to be of any challenge to such a villain as the Black Chicken. And truth be told, your companion looks to be a flashy dandy."

Still chortling, he pulled out a large blade from one of his sleeves and shook it at us.

"'Tis my judgement ye two are naught but a pair of jesters."

He stopped laughing and narrowed his eyes.

"Or are ye of that most perverse of professions, the bakers of tarts? Nay, prove yourselves or be gone from Medivus Rex in haste!"

Boneman made to pull his boot dagger, but it refused to come out of its sheath. Craithlbert started laughing again.

"Ungainly fool, thou canst not even fetch forth yer weapon. Ye certainly must be a – "

I jumped quickly – the gatekeeper found the Quonietzi pressed against his throat. I bared my canines close to his alarmed face.

"That's *Mr.* Tidley, thou miserable old curmudgeon. Drop the blade now or prepare to bleed over your scrolls."

Craithlbert's weapon clattered on the desktop.

Boneman finally retrieved his dagger.

"Got stuck, is all. Could have happened to anybody. Anyway, we got you now, old cur...curr...what Mr. Tidley said."

He reached inside his bright crimson vest and brought forth a square disk which he tossed on Craithlbert's desk.

"I sure hope you got a reader. That's my warrant for capture of the Chicken."

The geld collector looked at me. I nodded, and he picked up the disk. He moved some scrolls aside and inserted it into a slot by a small viewscreen on his desk. After a moment he retrieved the disk and tossed it back to Boneman.

"This of course makes the matter completely different."

I removed my dagger from his throat and sprang back next to Boneman. Craithlbert stared at me in wonder.

"I misjudged you and that is a fact, *Mr.* Tidley. Ye are, I ween, a true professional, as quick as the devil himself. I prithee, accept my humblest of apologies for my previous actions."

"Accepted," I said sheathing my dagger. "Now please tell us of this villain we seek."

The gatekeeper sighed.

"The Black Chicken appeared in this hall as if by

magic. He ripped my predecessor apart before the stunned man could send the alarm. The villain escaped out of Port Hrothgar and soon revealed himself as a foul conjurer and corrupter of the common weal. He sits in his high black castle, which is defended by the odious Dung Knight. Any who come for his master must attempt to best the knight in single combat. The warrior is unparalleled in his swordplay, all who have come to contest him have met the same fate. When the knight subdues a foe, a foul amulet of the Black Chicken's conjuring is forced upon on their neck. The defeated become mindless slaves tilling his lands, or laboring on additions to his castle. Most, however, are compelled to perform the most foul of duties – the baking of tarts!"

The geld collector sighed. "Medivus Rex is sparse populated, ruled by small baronies, earldoms, and dukedoms. No one has the will to attempt to dislodge the knave, so he sits conjuring and increasing his holdings. I fear that the day may come when he turns his slaves from laboring to make war against us all."

I said, "What does this Chicken look like?"

Craithlbert shrugged. "Alas, none who have seen the devil have ever returned, they lie dead or toil as his servants. That is all the information I have for thee. Now be welcome to Medivus Rex, ye may now purchase coins of the realm."

He pushed a button on his desk and on the left wall, a vestibule opened to reveal a boxy unit bearing the name *CelCred Exchange*. I walked up to it and punched buttons. After a few clicks and whirs a variety of gold and silver coins spewed from a slot into the bag I had ready. Boneman repeated the same action, and the wall slid shut again. The gatekeeper pulled a lever and the great oak door behind him slowly opened.

Craithlbert said, "Two of your trade have only but arrived and are now being outfitted by the armorer. If you hurry, you may meet them before they journey forth."

He stood and bowed to us.

"I wish you luck and good hunting. If you do succeed, you will not only gain your bounty but will also have titles and lands bestowed upon you here for ridding us of this baneful wizard. Be off now, pass through the gate and know that once through any modern devices shall not deign to function."

We walked into the doorway which opened to a bricked tunnel lit by more torches. As we came to the end of it, I felt a slight tickle over my entire body, it made the hackles on my backside raise up.

Boneman gave a shudder.

"Dang, what was that? Gave me goosebumps all over."

I said, "That was the tech-damper field, I would expect. I certainly hope you are well versed in weapons of the archaic style."

"Don't you worry about me," Boneman said with a scowl.

The tunnel gave way to a large cobblestone courtyard where there were many people hurrying about, all dressed in the manner of the planet's medieval style, you know, robes, pantaloons, chain mail, funny hats, and some very long and pointy footwear. There were lots of horses with riders, draft animals pulling carts, and a wide variety of smaller fowl and livestock – my delicate sense of smell was immediately assailed by it all. I spotted an open doorway with a hammer and a sword above it.

"That must be our next stop," said Boneman, "Gotta get ourselves the proper accou...uh, accutramans?"

"That would be accoutrements, Bonehead. Yes, that is the armorer's establishment. Let us hope he has something fitting for a Hundogca of House Jacks Russell."

We entered and were immediately greeted by a rather large human specimen with a bushy black beard. He wore a long leather apron that covered most of his bare, heavily muscled upper torso.

"Be ye welcome to the best outfitter in Port Hrothgar."

He made a low bow.

"Tulligan Flyspeck at your service, sirs, purveyor of arms and goods to those who would come to venture forth into merry Meddy Rex."

We made our perfunctory introductions and got down to business with Flyspeck. From his large rack he brought Boneman a broadsword, a two-piece bit of armor for his upper torso and a pair of amusing riveted steel pants with articulated metal shoes. All of that was topped off by an iron helm with a long feather plume in the center. After he was decked out, Boneman clanked and jingled like an ancient, doddering Stozbot – I let out a chortle.

The Boneman's face turned as red as his vest.

"I don't need all this extra stuff weighing me down, especially this danged tin suit."

He stripped off the hardware – despite the vigorous protests of Flyspeck – and from the armorer's rack chose a silver-bossed linden shield plus a lighter sword contained in a leather sheath that would strap to his back.

The outfitter threw up his arms, turned to me and squinted.

"You, sir, present me with a quandary. I have no plate

or mail that will suffice for you, let alone a shield, halberd, or the like. How can you go abroad in the land without protection?"

He scratched at his beard – after a moment his eyes lit up.

"I daresay that I do have something that mayhap will suit."

He turned and went through a curtained doorway. After a bit he returned holding a small crossbow and a quiver full of bolts. He also produced a needle-sharp thrusting poignard that had an incredible balance in my paw.

I said, "Yes, both items will do quite well for me."

Flyspeck rubbed at his hairy armpit.

"I will also provide ye with food, a map, and other such supplies as ye'll require for the road, including the use of me donkey, Balk, to bear it all. Be assured, young masters, he is of the most obedient nature and possesses a few rare talents."

After some haggling over prices – where I had to bare my canines more than once – we settled the monetary end of things.

"Ye have fleeced poor old Tully Flyspeck well," he said, scratching his behind.

"Ah, but enough o' that, ye'll be wanting food and drink now before ye go off for your quest. Best place for that is me cousin Wilt Farley's tavern, *The King's Rear*. 'Tis not but a couple of streets over from here off Falling Garter Alley."

After giving us directions, he said, "Here now, ye may leave Balk and yer supplies safely with me and pick all up after ye are refreshed."

The King's Rear had a sign overhead depicting a

flamboyantly dressed man with a crown sitting atop a rearing spotted horse – not at all what I had conjured up in my imagination. Familiar sounds of drunken revelry emanated from within as we approached the open door – it brought back memories of my old establishment on Guillaume 9, *The Sinking Pilgrim*. Ah well, that was all over and done with; the *Pilgrim* was nothing but flitzing ashes now.

The inn was smoky and dimly lit; other than a couple of oil lamps hanging from wooden beams the main illumination emanated from a few logs burning in a large hearth which was surrounded by a number of wooden chairs. Two of the chairs were occupied by humans I instantly recognized from past dealings – Ux Wanker and Wilhemina Hackblade, two of the best bounty hunters in the known universe.

Oh twaddle, I thought, *we have some very stiff competition now.* I told Boneman to get us some ale, then made my way across the rush covered floor to the hearth and took a seat close to the fire. Both bounty hunter's eyes widened when they saw me, but no hands went for weapons, which was a bit relieving. I believed I was on good terms with Hackblade. Ux Wanker...not so much.

Wilhemina broke into a broad smile, got up and came over to give me a big bear hug, which I reluctantly allowed.

"Why you broke down old Hundogca," she said, sitting down. "I thought you had gone off to one of the frontier worlds to live a quiet life as an innkeeper or some such flitzing thing."

She paused for a long pull on her mug of ale, and after a loud belch said, "Is it here you are living now? I wouldn't have thought Medivus Rex to be your style, if you will pardon my saying, old friend."

I replied, "It is pleasing to see you still looking relatively all in one piece Willi."

I noticed Wanker running an index finger over the long, deep scar on his face. He was not looking particularly happy to see me.

I said, "I hope we have no grievance with each other after all this time, Ux. It was never my intention to scar you so, but you seemed quite intent on ending me at the time, so – "

He snarled, "You should have cut my damned throat rather than my face, Tidley. Think that the years might have softened me, eh? Not a chance, I still hold my grudge and I'll not let it go so easily." His hand moved towards a large double-headed axe by his chair.

"It is *Mr.* Tidley, Wanker, and I would not raise that axe if I were you. My associate would not appreciate having to forgo his draught of ale just to forestall your effort of killing me."

"That's dang right," said Boneman standing directly behind Wanker, "Don't be making any moves to hurt my partner."

Ux hesitated, turned his head and looked him up and down.

"Who the hell are you?"

Boneman put down the two mugs of ale he was holding.

"I'm called The Boneman. Ya got that?"

He patted the hilt of the sword he wore on his back for emphasis.

"Me and Mr. Tidley are business associates, like he said, and I don't want nobody messing with my associate."

Ux turned back to me and laughed.

"When did you start taking up with greenhorns, Tidley? *Boneman?* What kind of moniker is that? Never heard a no Boneman. Looks more like some jumped up amateur ta me."

"I ain't no darn greenhorn," exclaimed Boneman, "and I don't like your attitude, furrow-face."

Ux sputtered in anger – he grabbed the axe. I drew the Quonietzi. Boneman made to pull his sword, but it stubbornly stuck in the sheath. At the same moment Wilhemina jumped up and rocked Wanker's chin with her ham-like fist. He collapsed in his chair with a crash.

"That'll be enough of that," she said wiping her hand as if it were coated with slime. "Ol' Ux is a mean-spirited plottskank, and that's a fact, but he has a few redeeming qualities. Besides I need him for the business we have here."

I replaced the Quonietzi while Boneman kept tugging at his sword.

I asked, "And what business might that be, Wilhemina?"

"We're going to bring in that there Black Chicken and collect the nice fat payday offered by CUPIES Central, and the gold the locals here are adding to the pot."

I nodded. "I see. Well, it seems like we may have a minor conflict then."

She frowned slightly.

"You don't live here then, do you? Damn it, Oswald, you're here for the same reason we are."

I winced – few knew my first name, let alone used it in public.

"Please Wilhemina. It is *Mr.* Tidley here. Yes, we have the same goal, but be assured my associate and I will abide by the Hunter's Code – you have arrived before us and therefore will get first opportunity at The Chicken. We will not impede or hinder you. Unless, of course, we find the brigand before you and Ux."

She grinned.

"Well that is as fair a deal as I could expect Ozzy...I mean, *Mr.* Tidley."

She stood up and proceeded to heft the unconscious Wanker over her shoulder.

"Heard some pretty wild stories about that knight defending the Black...oh hell, I'm just gonna call him the BC. Anyway, I hear that knight ain't been beaten by anyone who comes calling for his boss. Hell of a name too, Dung Knight, that's one unflattering title."

She turned to look at Boneman who had just ripped his sword free of its confinement.

"I don't know where you picked this one up, but good luck with him."

She gave me a wink.

"Well, best be off and away. I hope you get lost along the way, at least until after Ux and I have bagged the BC. No offense."

"None taken, Willi. Take diligent care of yourself."

She strode out the door with Wanker on her broad shoulder.

Boneman re-sheathed his weapon and took a long pull of his ale. He sat down, handed a mug to me and grinned.

"Well, Ozzy, that was a close shave. Who were those two anyway? That Wilhemina is one fast and strong lady, that's for sure. She sure put out that ugly fella's lights quick."

I took a long draught of the ale and then gave him an icy stare.

"Let us get one thing straight right now. It is Mr. Tidley to you until I tell you differently. Understand?"

He frowned but nodded in the affirmative.

"Good. Yes, Wilhemina Hackblade is remarkably able, and most certainly quite deadly when it comes to her trade as a bounty hunter. Many who thought otherwise are now ghostly memories. Ux Wanker is in the same line of work – good at what he does – not what I would call an honorable person at all. I find it quite curious they are working together."

I regarded The Boneman for a moment.

"Well, we have our work cut out for us. If they get to the BC before we do our journey to this backwater orbit will have been in vain. Let's get some food and then be off."

We ate a meal of steaming hot stew served up on large trenchers of bread, and then retrieved our donkey and supplies from Flyspeck's establishment. Flyspeck gave us a map to guide us to our goal and bade us farewell. We passed through a massive gate with a raised iron portcullis. The castle's high stone walls were surrounded by a large moat which was spanned by a drawbridge. As we crossed, I looked down and saw the moat was inhabited by some very large, scaly, reptiles. One of them looked up at me with red eyes and hissed, opening a wide mouth filled with wicked teeth the size of pickaxes. *Ancestors to the Umvornians?* I thought. *No, cannot be. These creatures are much better looking and don't have speech that sounds like a herd of flatulent Titan buffaloes.*

After we crossed, Balk decided that was as far as he wanted to venture – he sat down and refused to move. I cursed the damn thing as a plinktwaddler and misbegotten offspring of a Clavvish worm rustler to no avail. Boneman used similar expletives followed by several boots to its rear, but the beast remained stubbornly rooted.

I finally had a thought and reached into one of the packs lashed to the donkey. I walked around and held a nice red apple in front of Balk's muzzle. His ears pricked up; he stood, quickly walking towards me. I retreated, he followed. Problem solved.

The road we followed – interrupted with many sit-down strikes by the obstinate Balk – took us through cultivated fields of corn and grains and eventually led under the canopy of a dark forest. It was close and eerily quiet as we walked along, no birdsong nor chittering of squirrels. The only sounds were that of our plodding along and occasional creaking of the massive gnarled trees that surrounded the road on both sides. It was quite hot, so I removed my pantaloons and vest in favor of a belted breechclout. I kept the dagger at my belt and poignard sheathed on my back.

We reached a turn in the road and came to an abrupt halt. Standing before us was a being who looked, well, like a four-meter tall bundle of sticks and assorted flora. It regarded us with a single eye that resembled a large razzle berry. The thing waved a branchy arm at us.

"I am Herbert, a creature of twigs and bracken, defender of sprouts, certain nuts, and small fruits. You may not proceed further on this road."

Boneman stepped forward.

"Hey there, Mr. Sticks. What's the problem?"

The being shook all over, causing dust and little flowers to fall from its body.

"I am *Herbert*, not *Mr. Sticks*. Do not trifle with me, for I am a mighty elemental being who may cause you all manner of dread. You may not go further because there are newborns on the road who may not be disturbed."

He gestured to a swath of green covering the road behind him.

"See my wonderful little charges. Never fear, soon a new bypass will soon be constructed by the officials at Port Hrothgar and should be completed by mid-winter. For now, you may backtrack and take the high mountain road."

I started to protest when Balk slipped his rope, charged past Herbert and began nibbling on the greenery.

Herbert screamed, "Murderer! Quit eating and stepping on my little darlings, you foul creature."

He swatted Balk on the rump to no avail. Herbert picked the donkey up with his branch arms and held him close to his face.

"You will pay for this. I will – "

Balk took a large chomp out of Herbert's face. With a reedy scream the woody creature dropped the donkey and clutched its munched face.

"My eye, the monster has eaten beautiful my eye! Oh, I will deal you a horrid blow for this, you vile, four-legged, ratty-furred cousin to a mule deer. Come here so I may crush you into muck!"

He began stomping around blindly with large rooty feet. Balk took a bite out of one of his twiggy legs. With a roar of pain, the bundle of sticks hopped away and disappeared into the forest crying, "Nobody respects the elementals anymore."

I retrieved Balk's rope and gave him a little pat on the muzzle.

Boneman said, "Dang, ol' Balk took care of that twiggy character. Good boy! Well, it's getting late. Maybe we ought to set up camp here. I don't think we'll get any more trouble from ol' blind Mr. Sticks now, and Balk sure loves them greens. What do you think?"

"Yes, a fine idea. Though I hope Balk doesn't overdo it with the rich food."

We started out early in the morning after passing an uneventful night in the forest. Balk seemed quite bloated and walked even slower than the previous day. We came through the wood into green fields which gave way to rolling hills. A towering black castle occupied the highest of them.

I turned to Boneman.

"Our destination, and I sincerely hope that we have arrived before our competition."

"Yeah, me too," he replied. "Let's make some tracks up there and get us some Chicken."

We followed the road as it wound through emerald green meadows and recently harvested fields before it began rising into the hills. I could see people in the distance harvesting wheat. After a time, we came to a small hamlet where the inhabitants were carrying on with their day-to-day labors. I thought something was very strange about them, and it finally dawned on me – their lurching gait, and –

Boneman hailed one who bore a hamper of wheat on his shoulder.

"Hey there, good sir, is that there castle up ahead owned by a fella called Black Chicken?"

The man paid no heed, swayed past us and went into a thatched storehouse to deposit his load.

"Damn unfriendly lot," said Boneman, "Don't believe we're gonna get answers here."

I replied, "No, I think we will not, and I believe I know why. Look at his neck."

The man came lurching out of the storehouse and walked past Boneman towards a nearby field of tall wheat. Boneman turned back to me, mouth agape.

"Goddamn. What the hell is that on his throat? Looks like some kinda black metal starfish."

I said, "It is a controlling device, and it resembles more a chicken foot than a starfish. I have seen something similar before."

I informed Boneman of a brief stop I had made at the prison orbit Ouunus Minor where I saw such apparatus employed on its unfortunate inmates. All had that vacant look in their eyes as they shuffled and lurched along to toil in the factories that produced the highly toxic desserts, Winkies and Bing-Bongs. The rectangular mechanisms attached to their necks were Altus 3 regulators – highly illegal on any human or CUPIES orbit.

"It must have been altered by the BC to appear as a household sigil, or brand. How narcissistic of the villain. I am puzzled as to how can it function with the damper field and computer grid?"

Boneman nodded. "Yeah. How can that be?"

"Never mind that now. I believe we have just met one of the Dung Knight's failed challengers. He is now apparently under the control of the BC, and has become one of the local labor forces, just as the Gatekeeper informed us."

"Dang, too bad he wasn't one of them who makes the tarts. I could use me some of that right about now."

I said, "It will be prudent to be watchful now. All the people here and in the fields are likely under his control."

We left the village and continued in the direction of the castle. The road led us down into a valley then back up to where it ventured into the black maw of a tunnel.

I said, "I certainly hope our adversary is not lurking in there."

Boneman lit a torch and we entered. The tunnel was quite dark beyond the light our torch cast, its mossy walls seeped water that trickled into our path. Balk's stomach grumbled loudly and echoed off the dank walls After about an hour of trudging we saw light looming ahead. My hackles went up suddenly, I stopped and turned around. We were being followed.

It appeared to be a horde of wraiths – wispy, with a gauzy look – kind of dream-like until you got to the faces. They had huge bulging eyes and wide mouths that were full of razor-like teeth – a lot of teeth. They were about ten meters or so behind us and closing rapidly.

I said, "We need to move faster, right now. Look behind us, Boneman."

The Boneman turned and his eyes bulged out in horror. He started to run. I pulled and prodded Balk, but to no avail. The flitzing tinkwaddler of a donkey decided it was time to go on strike again and stood rock solid in place. The floating horrors were almost upon us. I could hear them mewling with anticipation as their mouths opened even wider.

I was about to drop Balk's rope and run like a five-legged vorbit runner with its buttocks on fire, when Balk raised his tail. BLAMMMORGH!!! He let go with the loudest and longest rump-roar I had ever heard.

It was as if a gale force had hit the wraiths. They were literally blown away to ghostly fragments – wailing in indignation – that were sucked into the tunnel's moldy walls. I was quite glad to have not been on the receiving end of Balk's gaseous salvo. I pulled on the rope with an apple in my other paw and Balk came along willingly. *Tully Flyspeck was right about one thing*, I thought, *Balk does possess a few rare talents.*

The tunnel came out on top of a hill. We began to descend the path which wove down into a small valley with a river flowing through. At the other end of the valley, on a larger hill, was the castle. When we were almost down, I could see that there was a narrow stone bridge spanning the river with three people upon it. Two were Wanker and Hackblade, the third – who stood in their way – was a lone knight.

Boneman came up next to me and looked at the trio below.

"Hey, that must be the Dung Knight. That damn bridge is so narrow they can only come at him one at a time."

Hackblade approached the knight with her broadsword ready. When she got within about ten feet of him, she began to sway and with her free hand tried to cover her nose. The knight waited with his sword lowered as Wilhemina wavered on. I could hear her cry out, "Twaddle it all, the smell!" She made a two-handed swing with her heavy blade.

The knight moved swiftly. In an instant he struck the broadsword from her hand. With a backhand sweep, he slapped her head with the flat of his sword. She collapsed at the knight's feet.

Ux Wanker gave a guttural cry and came at the knight quickly with his huge double-headed axe. As he got closer, he too became shaky, but staggered onwards. He met a similar fate as his partner. The knight moved, parried the axe and struck Wanker with his mailed fist – he dropped like a sack of soggy plogtworts.

The knight turned towards the black castle and waved his sword over his head. Within a few moments two huge ravens swirled up from behind its dark walls and sped towards him. The ravens came to rest on the bridge's stone railings; each held a dark object in their beaks which they offered to the knight. He accepted the items then quickly placed them on Hackblade and Wanker's necks.

Boneman and I watched in amazement as both Wanker and Hackblade slowly stirred then rose up. Well, I suppose we shouldn't have been too surprised – the old gatekeeper did tell us about this after all – but still, it was pretty flitzing amazing. The ravens flew off to where they had come – the bounty hunters followed, lurching past the knight without a word.

"Dang. Did you see that? Hope ol' Ux won't be serving up tarts with that ugly face," said Boneman.

I was speechless. The two bounty hunters were considered among the best of their trade; to see them so quickly and decisively defeated was unnerving to say the least. In my mind I had a picture of Wilhemina Hackblade serving baked goods in her new master's castle. *Her spirit would be spitting nails about the unjustness of it all*, I thought.

I finally said, "Flitz, that knight is endowed with extreme skill to be able to defeat those two. We must have a plan."

"Well ain't no sense just sittin' up here and moaning,"

Boneman said. "Let's get on down there and check things out closer."

We made our way down the hill and approached the bridge. I said, "I shall be the one to first engage the Knight."

"Ah, come on Mr. Tidley, you gotta let me do it. That guy is way too big for you to take on by yourself."

I snarled, "Don't ever underestimate my size. You do remember who saved you from that large Orgl back on Guillaume 9?"

Just then Balk decided to stage another protest and stopped in his tracks. I sighed and went back to fetch another apple out of the pack. I also grabbed my crossbow that was tied to the beast. When I turned back, I beheld Boneman on the bridge walking towards the knight.

Forgetting Balk, I slung the crossbow, quickly dropped to all fours and ran towards my foolish partner who was now tugging at the sword on his back. I could tell I would not make it in time and stopped at the foot of the bridge. I could smell the reason why the knight was so named – the odorous perfume evoked something primal that made me want to roll all over him in great joy.

Boneman got closer – the knight hailed him.

"What ho? Who dares approach the environs of my master, The Black Chicken?"

Boneman covered his nose and gagged a reply.

"I'm The Boneman, and I come here to take the old Chicken back to CUPIES for justice and get the reward for the danged villain. Whew, you smell like to a herd of clittered blink's three-day-old droppings. Guess that's why you got the name of Dung Knight, eh?"

The knight shook his sword.

"This foul stench which rolls off my person, though

indecorous, is far a better fate than the baking of tarts. You, I ween, shall make a fine purveyor of the dainty pastries after I have bested you."

Boneman came at him, weapon drawn.

"Come on, stinky. I'm gonna slice and dice you back into little cow-pies."

He took another reeling step and fainted.

Suppressing my urge to roll all over the knight, I raised my crossbow and let loose a bolt. The shaft struck him directly in the middle of the chest with a *plunk*, which caused him to falter for a moment. I dropped the bow and ran at him full speed – stabbing him with my poignard in the upper thigh – and scooted between his legs to the other side of the bridge.

"Take that, foul Dung-beetle. Thou hast the visage of a knight, but ye are naught but a pile of magic excrement!"

The stink was overwhelming to me, but I was able to control myself and mock him. He turned away from Boneman, apparently unaffected by the wounds I'd inflicted on him. He clanked towards me, sword at the ready.

"Come hither and fight, ye furred creature of small stature. What manner of demon art thou to have such ears and snout?"

I laughed.

"A demon such as you have never encountered, odious crumpet from a bovine's behind."

I ran between his legs again and slashed at his calf on the way. Now I was in front of the Boneman. The knight whirled around with his sword held high.

"Hold ye still and fight me with honor, little imp."

"I shall fight you on my terms, Turd Knight. You will

have no more victims to send to your lord, for this day I will dispatch you, Sir Flatulence."

He became visibly agitated and shook his sword violently.

"Stop, I prithee, thy speech is full of mockery and 'tis not fair to me. I am bound to serve my master, compelled to subdue all who would take him. I do not claim to take joy from the deeds, but I am controlled by his sorcery. Have mercy on me, diminutive fiend; stand and fight."

I snarled and flicked the Quonietzi at his chest. As he moved to deflect it, I took another run at him and stabbed him in the gut. The knight was unaffected; with a twitch of his sword he disarmed me and booted me back to where the Boneman lay moaning. I tried to bring up Boneman's sword, but it was too heavy for me.

The Dung Knight stood over me.

"Prepare to meet thy fate worthy adversary. There hath been none who have struck me with a weapon afore – yet ye have done so thrice. I bemoan the idea of you making tarts and other baked goods for my accursed master, but I must dispatch you now with much regret."

He raised his mailed fist to strike.

I ducked between his legs, turned and saw a black sigil on his right heel. I did the last thing I could think of as my final act of defiance; I lifted my leg and urinated on the device.

"I pisseth on you and the seal of your foul master of a Black Chicken!"

The sign of the Chicken sizzled and popped; the odorous warrior dropped his sword and began to totter and sway with mailed hands clasped to his helmed head. He shook vigorously, causing his armor to ring like a wonky string of out of tune wind chimes. With a final shake he became quite still.

He gasped, "What has happened to me? I have dim memories...yes, yes...I remember."

He knelt and looked at me closely.

"You shorted out his controller with your acidic pee, buddy. I sure owe you one...Mr?"

"Mr. Tidley. But if I broke the magic, should you not be but an inanimate pile of manure now, or at least dying from the wounds you have sustained?"

The knight raised his visor revealing a doughy face that had the consistency of...well never mind.

"No, no you got it all wrong. That damned Chicken abducted me off my home world, Schrecklicher Gestank, long ago. It's a world out in the uncharted territories, and as far as I know it's never been visited by anyone from off-planet until the Chicken came."

He stood up and shook his fist at the air.

"I was living the good life, fighting, feuding, and flower arranging. One day that hooded bastard appeared out of nowhere. When I saw him I was dumbstruck, I'd never seen anything like him before. Anyway, he grabbed me and placed that damnable device on my heel, which not only made me do his bidding, but also greatly enhanced my personal aroma. My weaponized odor usually did the trick in defeating my opponents, that is, until you came along, Mr. Tidley."

Now that he mentioned it, I did notice that my urge to roll all over him was now greatly reduced. The air about him, though still quite pungent, was bearable.

The Dung Knight did a twirl with both his arms outstretched.

"Now I'm free and I can talk right again too; boy is that good news. As to the wounds, well, let's just say my bodily composition doesn't react that way. What looks to you as armor is really kind of like an exoskeleton or carapace, it's all part of me. Hell, you'd need to chop me up into tiny pieces and burn 'em all up to really do me in."

He held out his hand.

"Name is Louie Twinkles, pleased ta meetcha!"

I reluctantly took it with my paw.

"Likewise, I'm sure."

Boneman sat up and shook his head. When he saw the knight, he jumped up with his sword ready.

"Okay Dung-boy, now I'm gonna cut you up into little poopy bon-bons."

I held up a paw.

"He is no longer our enemy. I have released him from the BC's control and as a result, his body odor has been significantly diminished."

Boneman hesitated, then lowered his sword.

"Well okay, he may be alright, but he still stinks pretty bad, burns my eyes a little too."

Lou pulled my crossbow bolt out of his chest and held out his hand to The Boneman.

"Twinkles, Louie Twinkles. Sorry about the smell, that kind of goes with the territory, but the Chicken has no more control over me and I don't smell near as bad now, thanks to Mr. Tidley here."

I watched as Boneman reluctantly shook hands with Louie the Dung Knight – former Dung Knight that is – and then wiped his hand on his breeches.

"Well dang, I guess your days of staying on this here bridge knocking people off are over, huh?"

Louie nodded vigorously.

"You can bet on that, pal. Now that I'm free I'm gonna settle with that damn Black Chicken."

He picked up his sword.

"Say, you two want to team up and go get him with me?"

I thought about it for a moment then, "I suppose that would be acceptable. Do you agree, Boneman? He has an unnatural ability in combat – that is, if it was not part of the BC's control program."

I quickly picked up the poignard and made to strike at Louie, who moved with unnerving speed to parry me.

"I'd say he still has it, alright," said my partner. "Yeah, I'm okay with him coming along, but what about the reward?"

I said, "I think a three-way split will be okay, after all the reward is quite a handsome sum – no one of us will go hungry."

Boneman nodded in agreement.

"I'm sure glad he doesn't smell as gawd-awful as he did. No offense Twinkles, but you did reek like splattered Blingie turds on a half loaf of Umvornian whizzy bread. Now it's more like pig-sty lite."

I shrugged.

"Yes, Louie is more bearable now. Now, with the three of us together we should make an easy job of cornering the BC."

Twinkles said, "That'd be really nice, but you oughtta know that he ain't so easy to capture. He's a damn cunning and slippery devil, definitely not what you would expect with those nasty, retractable, and sharp – "

Boneman laughed.

"Well, we'll see about that. We beat you after all."

I said, "You mean I did, Bonehead. Let's go retrieve the villain before he gets up to any more mischief."

We gathered our weapons and Balk, then took the winding road up to the black castle. Coming closer to the black walled stronghold I could see the gate was wide open. Suddenly there arose a great cacophony from within. I looked up to see a black swirl of ravens arising into the air and heading for us. At the gate stood a hooded figure, arms extended, with black-gloved hands gesturing at the black birds.

"It's the Chicken," said Louie the Dung Knight. He charged forward, sword held high. The ravens circled above him. We followed a bit more warily. Louie got within about ten meters of the Chicken when from the skies came a great erupting of raven poop that hit him with great accuracy, slowing him down and finally encasing him like a strange white and black crap statue; he moved no further.

Boneman exclaimed, "He got buried in bird turds! What a dang nasty way to go."

The ravens wheeled as one and turned their attention towards us. I grabbed my crossbow and let loose a bolt at the hooded figure commanding them. The arrow impacted him in the chest; he screeched loudly and staggered backwards. The ravens broke away and dispersed in all directions as if set free from an enchantment.

Old instincts kicked in and I rushed at the figure on all fours, canines bared. He reached out and flipped a wooden lever which dropped a heavy iron portcullis. I came skidding to a halt as it clanged down in front of me.

The figure threw back his hood and glared at me with feral slitted eyes. His tufted ears were flattened against the orange and black striped fur of his head. I recognized his species from the old hist-vids – Kattze.

He hissed, "Hundogca!"

I had another primal urge, this time to get down on all fours, chase the BC, then bite and shake him. *Where did that come from?* He was as big as Boneman, which was all out of whack with what the old holos had showed. Damnable thing should have been smaller than me.

"I thought you guys were long gone, like for thousands of years."

The Kattze pulled the bolt from a leather padded chest plate and cast it down on the ground.

"You are misinformed, tiny excuse for a dog. We escaped from CUPIES and found homes far away from their detestable empire. I see your kind have become lackeys to their rule. Just like you were with your former human masters – bootlickers, all of you."

"Oh, cut the flitzing twizzle talk," I said, now recovered from my initial shock. "What brings you back and how did you get so twaddling big?"

He sneered and spat.

"Unlike your kind, we took CUPIES Regen tank information with us and, shall we say, improved ourselves further. I have been exiled by my fellow Kattze for, what they considered, questionable business transactions. Perhaps there were a few deaths of highly-placed Kattze officials as well, but they were most assuredly accidents – nothing to do with me. As a result of these false charges I have been outlawed, branded with the distasteful title of Black Chicken. Now I am wanted by CUPIES and a score of other orbits for my... perfectly legitimate business dealings. I have a good thing going on this planet now, a great center of operations you might say, and you, little mongrel, will not upset that plan."

I snarled at him.

"The name is *Mr.* Tidley, you mange-affected plinktwaddler. I have read how your kind was quite haughty and overbearing, and now you are proving it true. Still pooping in boxes by the way? Nasty habit, that."

The Kattze's eyes slitted.

"Dare not speak to me in that way, leg-lifter-to-pee, or you will pay dearly."

Boneman came up beside me.

"Hey, they shoulda called you the Black Striped Kitty-Kat. Now come on out, fur-ball, and give up or we're gonna have to come in and take you the old rough and tumble way. The way you been spouting off to my friend Mr. Tidley, I kind of hope you do it the hard way."

The Kattze opened his eyes wide with fury; I thought steam would soon begin to come spouting out of his tufted ears. He ripped off his gloves and exposed wicked retractable claws.

"Impudent human. I shall rend your flesh and take your head so I may mount it on my wall as a trophy."

I had had enough of this, so I began wriggling between the bars of the iron gate, the poignard in my paw. The Chicken produced a Szkely M2 blaster from his sleeve and aimed it at me; with a clang, Boneman's sword reached through the grate and knocked it out of his paw. I flicked my dagger at the villain and it thumped into his unprotected thigh. He howled in pain and hobbled quickly into the castle courtyard. I got to the edge of the courtyard just as he punched a button on his belt – the Kattze shimmered and disappeared.

I went back and raised the portcullis enough for Boneman to stoop through. He picked up the Szkely and his eyes widened slightly.

He said, "This is charged and ready to fire. He would have crisped us for sure. How did he get that to work on Meddy Rex?"

"My question exactly, partner. Something is amiss."

We entered the courtyard and I saw many small box-like contraptions affixed to the stone walls and a large central cube in the center of the cobbled yard.

Boneman saw them and nodded.

"Those boxes and central unit are a Bax 5 field generator package. Dang, he must have created a radius around the castle that affected the computer grid and damper field. That explains why the Altus regulators worked on his laborers."

"And be able to do a teleport," I said.

I smelled a familiar odor, turned and beheld Louie Twinkles, the Dung Knight, looking a bit crusty and dappled in white.

"He got away? Damn. He's beamed up to the ship he has parked in orbit. He'll be on his way out of this sector at full speed. We'll have a heck of a time getting the furry critter now."

I said, "Well we had better get back to Port Hrothgar and make a start. Louie, I assume you are now a part of our motley crew?"

"It's an honor and a pleasure, Tidley."

"That's *Mr.* Tidley!"

We trudged back the way we had come to Port Hrothgar. Balk did not once go on strike during our return and instinctively guided us right to his stable at Tully

Flyspeck's. After leaving the donkey, we made our way to the spaceport gate.

"We'll have to inform the gatekeeper about the Kattze's breach of their damper field and grid," I said.

"Yeah, they'll be wanting to fix that right away," said Boneman. "I wonder if we are gonna get lands and titles for getting rid of the Chicken for them? I kinda would like to be a baron or duke and have tarts made for me."

He looked over at Louie and began to chuckle.

"What would your title be Louie? The Duke of Dung or the Earl of Excrement?"

I said, "This is no time to worry about being royalty on a backwards orbit like Medivus Rex." *Although the idea of running a tavern and gaming hall here does have a bit of rustic appeal*, I thought briefly.

We reached the gate and entered. I felt the slight electric shock of the field as I passed through.

The gatekeeper – holding his nose with Louie present – was incensed when we told him about the Chicken, but also quite glad to be rid of him. After imparting a rather large amount of gold and silver to us, he sat back in his chair and regarded us from under his bird-like brows.

"'Tis merry news the Chicken has left us, but it would be even merrier if you had brought his head on a pike. We will hasten men at arms and a few of our people who handle the technical matters to his castle and destroy his machines. We will also take care of the poor wretches he has enslaved. 'Tis my hope we will not need to urinate on them to remove the wretched amulets."

He paused and looked thoughtful.

"Port Hrothgar has need of one or two of them who might retain knowledge of the baking of tarts. It seems the populace has of late developed quite a yearning for the dainties. As to where he has bolted, I have transmitted the details to your ship's computer. He is journeying to territories wild, known to us only in tales and myth. It is said that fierce demons dwell there who are quite unsavory and hostile to any who dare to venture in. Mayhap that will be the end of the knave, and a fitting one at that."

He paused and then tossed a ribbon-bound scroll to each of us.

"Know ye now that ye all are hereby honorary knights of our realm. I dub thee Sir Tidley, Sir Boneman, and Sir Twinkles. If ever it is your desire to return to fair Medivus, know ye shall be received with great accord and reverence for ridding us of such a foul scoundrel."

He eyed Louie for a moment.

"Sir Twinkles, on behalf of all the population of Medivus Rex I beseech ye to find a place other than our fair planet. I mean no offense, but the truth of it is the odors that emanate from your person puts a man off his desire for tarts, if ye catch my meaning."

The Dung Knight nodded.

"No offense taken, yer worship, and not to worry. I am taking ship with my two comrades to pursue the villain."

Craithlbert gave a smile of relief.

"Go thee then in peace and may God protect ye on your quest."

We took off in *The Wilting Lily* and set a pursuit course; the ship's air filtration system worked a bit harder as it attempted to compensate for our new partner's eau de cologne. I was able to put away my instinct to roll all over him. Boneman took to wearing a small gas mask at times.

Weeks later Boneman called me over to the com.

"You got a message Sir...I mean *Mr.* Tidley."

Wilhemina Hackblade faced me with a grin.

"Hey, just want to thank you, Oswald, for getting me and Ux out of that fix on Med Rex."

"It was a pleasure, Willi, at least as far as you go. Where are you headed now?"

She cast her eyes downwards and blushed slightly.

"Well, truth is me and Ux are still here in Port Hrothgar. We decided that we might settle down for a spell, maybe get hitched...who knows? Anyway, we opened a little shop where Ux bakes tarts and I serve tea. The only stress that occurs now is when the occasional customer disparages one of Ux's creations and I have to hide his axe before he cuts their head off. He really is a very sensitive soul you know."

She cleared her throat; her eyes met mine.

"Old Craithlbert told me where you were heading, and I gotta tell you that you're in for flitzing trouble."

"What do you mean, Willi? You and I have known each other for a long time now. What trouble could possibly worry me?"

Her image began to flicker.

"I have run the data on the Kattze's course and he is heading directly to Ploggiss Umvor. Ozzy, you know what that is... the home world of the Umvornians."

The com screen flickered again and went blank.

A large knot started to grow in my stomach. *Umvornians?* I began to have a feeling that my adventure on Medivus Rex would be nothing compared to what might be in store for us next.

ABOUT THE AUTHOR

Alex Starke lives with his wife, Anne, and four Jack Russell terriers in Eugene, Oregon. He is a graduate of the University of Oregon with a degree in Medieval Studies and a minor in Early Modern European History. He currently is doing fine art photography and just living the dream.